WICCAN DREAM

TRACI HALL

"Well developed characters, an accurate portrayal of psychic abilities, an intriguing plot combined with teen angst will keep you reading this book into the night. Traci Hall has created a wonderful protagonist in Rhiannon Godfrey and wonderful secondary characters. Now I have to read the rest of the series!
– Melissa Alvarez, *author and intuitive clairvoyant*

"As always, Ms. Hall manages to beautifully convey real characters--and the human emotion that rules us through all time. I love her work!"
– Heather Graham, *New York Times Bestselling Author of* PHANTOM EVIL

"Traci Hall writes with gripping emotion and engaging twists, whether it's for teens or adults, Ms. Hall pens a fabulous tale!"
– Cherry Adair, *New York Times Bestselling Author of KISS and* TELL

"Traci Hall brings ALL the issues of being a teenager to life through Rhee, her friends, and her magical family. The balance of Wiccan beliefs and psychic powers kept me reading into the early morning hours, reminding me of my trials as young woman, studying Wicca and managing the ability to see spirits. A great read for young and old alike!!"
– Ginger Quinlan, *Certified Psychic Medium, Author*

"Traci Hall is a magical storyteller!"
– Rhonda Pollero, *USA Today bestselling author*

"A new talent to watch!"
– Amy J. Fetzer

"No one does teenage angst like Traci Hall… It's a paranormal feast at warp speed!"
– Michael Meeske, *Author of FRANKENSTEIN'S DAEMON*

ACKNOWLEDGEMENTS

This book wouldn't have been finished without the belief of my readers. J.W., thank you for your encouragement, and Jennifer B, you are a shining star. Thanks to Twyla DiGangi for her magic spell!

Mom, Brighton, Destini, Sheryl, Chris and MM - xoxoxo

CHAPTER ONE

"Rhiannon!" Melody's voice trembled with excitement despite it being the crack of dawn on a Saturday.

"What?" Ten in the morning felt way too early to be awake.

"It's the hot delivery guy from Box It."

Rhiannon looked up from her tower of Jelly Bean candles (scented, not shaped) that arrived yesterday with the other stock for Celestial Beginnings.

The New Age shop her mother had started at the back of the property did surprisingly well in small town Crystal Lake, Washington. All of the drama since her family had moved here helped sales.

Her dad liked to say that there was no such thing as bad publicity.

"So, go unlock the door." Rhiannon picked her way through the maze of merchandise. Heaping mounds of handcrafted afghans, baskets of homeopathic lotions and artfully arranged pyramids of candles helped the shopper completely forget that cows used to do cow things in this old barn. *Ugh*.

Melody took a sip of her peppermint mocha, brown eyes sparkling. "How old do you think he is? Twenty, twenty-one?"

"Thirty?" Rhiannon laughed at Melody's crestfallen expression. "Perfect for your average high school crush."

"That's practically ancient!" Melody swept the keys into her palm and marched toward the front door. "And I don't have a crush." She peeked out the side window before sticking the key in the lock. "He's too adorable to be thirty, Rhee."

"I could be wrong. Let him in before he drops that heavy looking box and I'll check for crow's feet."

With a low un-Melody-like giggle, she opened the door. Mr. Hot Box It grinned and entered, sprinkles of rain sliding down his uniform jacket and off a dark curl over his forehead.

"Morning, ladies," he said. "Which one of you is Rhiannon Godfrey?"

"I am," Rhee answered, curious.

"This is a special delivery." He set the box on the counter and whipped out a clipboard. After eyeing Rhee from head to toe, he gave a friendly nod. "Your signature only. Should I check for ID?" Wink.

"We're only sixteen," Melody said, studying his face. "Why would you need identification?"

Rhiannon blushed at her friend's reminder of their age and reached for the pen he held out. "I didn't order anything. Where is this from?"

He read the invoice. "J.W.'s Magic Emporium."

A thrill made her shiver. "I've never heard of that," Rhiannon said. She handed the pen and clipboard back, then looked at the box. About the size of a case of computer paper, wrapped in brown, with a giant Box It stamp on the side. "Does it list what's in it?"

"Nope." The cute delivery guy headed to the door. "Special instructions were that you personally had to sign for the box. That's it."

"What if it's dangerous?" Melody asked, concern in her voice.

He paused by the door and gave them a grin that promised no worries. "Box It guarantees every delivery. If there's a problem, call the store." He took a business card from his coat pocket and handed it to Melody with another wink. "Or you could just call me." He left, the door closing behind him with the clink of bells attached to the knob.

Rhiannon elbowed her friend. "Call me?"

Mel's smile filled her entire face. "If there's a problem..."

"Whatever!" Rhee shook her head. "He might be twenty three-ish. Which is still too old for you. Besides, Caleb might not appreciate his girlfriend drooling over other guys."

Melody gave a last look out the window at the delivery truck's taillights. "Me and Caleb are over. For good this time."

Rhiannon sent a wave of empathy Mel's direction. "I'm sorry. Right before Valentine's Day?"

"My choice. Let's leave it at that."

Melody's prickly exterior hid a soft underbelly, so Rhiannon nodded, determined to find out more later. "Okay."

Mel gave the box a push but it didn't budge. "This is heavy. Are you going to open it, or what?"

Rhee rubbed her arms. "I'm pretty positive I didn't order anything. And Mom wouldn't ask for a delivery with my signature. That makes no sense."

"Maybe it's got something to do with your people at the Institute." Melody wore her thick brown hair in two braids on either side of her face, and she tugged at the end of one as if nervous. Despite her grandmother being a shaman, Mel didn't care for the mystical.

"My people? We're paranormal scientists, not another race." Rhee crossed her arms in thought. "Maybe, though." The Institute of Parapsychology in Las Vegas, Nevada had been home as she learned about her paranormal talents.

She and her family moved to Washington after an episode where Rhee had used her gifts to hurt another girl. With what she felt was good reason, though her parents disagreed.

Leading to her being stuck in the middle of nowhere so Rhiannon could learn to be normal. "Normal never did work out."

"Huh?" Melody narrowed her eyes.

"Never mind." Rhee blew out a slow breath and concentrated on the box. What was inside? She focused, telepathically delving past the layers of cardboard and paper. Plastic. More paper.

"Ouch!" She jerked back as she hit a psychic barrier, pressing the bridge of her nose. It was like walking into a glass door.

"Are you okay?"

"Yes." Rhiannon touched the moonstone pendant she wore beneath her sweater. "Something magickal is in that box. And there are shields around it. Protecting it?"

Melody took a step backward, accidentally knocking over the basket of rainbow-colored fanged kittens. Stuffed, of course. "Woops."

Rhee waited until Mel had put the popular toys back, then asked to borrow her box cutter. "I'm going to burn some sage, too, just in case it's dark magick."

"Maybe you should wait for your mom before you open it."

Rhiannon graced Mel with an arched brow to do her mother proud. "Have I or have I not managed to clear ghosts from this very farmhouse? I can handle a box without any help." She held out her palm, and Mel reluctantly handed over the blade.

"I'm just saying."

Rhiannon lit a sage candle with a directed thought, then tucked her hair behind her ear and whispered a prayer for guidance to the Goddess. She said over her shoulder to Mel, "You might want to step back."

With a decisive slice of the blade, Rhiannon cut the tape from the box. A musty stench escaped the mess of bubble wrap and wadded up newspaper. She brought her knuckles to her mouth. "Yuck."

"What is that stink? Mom hit a skunk once on the freeway at night that smelled almost as bad as this." Melody plugged her nose and peered inside, hands tucked close to her body so she didn't touch something gross.

"Nothing dead, I hope. Here." She handed the blade to Mel and carefully brushed aside the packing materials. "There must be something fragile."

The small hairs on the back of her neck rose once her fingers connected with a solid object. She pulled it free of the box, noticing two similar items at the bottom. "It's heavy. Like a rock. Why would a shop send me a freaking rock? Do you realize what it must have cost to ship?"

"I don't like this." Melody exhaled a peppermint mocha breath. "Your mom could be here in two minutes."

Rhiannon peeled back the wrappings to reveal a mostly nude stone statue the size of her forearm.

Melody tucked both hands in the back pockets of her jeans. "Ugh. Who is that?"

"Got me." The marbled figure had black wings and carried a wand. Chipped in places, it emitted low energy that made Rhee's hand tingle.

"Nice fig leaf," Melody snickered.

Rhee tried to give Melody the statue, but her friend backed up and shook her head.

"No thanks. It's creepy."

"Agreed." Rhiannon set the statue upright on a small table next to the stuffed kittens. "But look at the detail. You can see every wave of his hair. And those are the Wizard of Oz flowers on his wand thing."

"Poppies."

"Yeah. They made Dorothy sleep, remember?" She felt a tickle at the nape of her neck.

"Drugged by the evil witch."

"There are no evil witches here, Mel. Just the good kind." She reached inside the box for the other two objects, which turned out to be similar statues, though the first one had more humanistic traits. "Wings – they could be the flying monkeys, except for the fangs. Kinda cute."

"Only you would find fangs cute. I'm guessing you ordered the stuffed kittens, too."

"They sell out faster than we can keep them in stock."

Rhiannon brushed her hands against her jeans then lifted an envelope and a framed document. "This looks like a certificate." Her heart beat faster as she realized what she was looking at then her stomach rolled as she stared at the statues.

"What?" Melody put her hand to Rhee's shoulder.

"I could have dropped them." She swallowed and met Mel's gaze. "These should be in a museum or something. Marble statues of the Oneiroi, dating from 200 A.D."

Melody looked horrified. "And I thought thirty was old."

CHAPTER TWO

Rhee emptied the box. "There's a letter, to me. Here, help me with this one. It's not like they bite."

"That you know of." Melody reluctantly took the sleeping winged statue.

Rhiannon gently carried the other two along with the letter to the couches before the electric fireplace. She and Melody set the statues down on the coffee table.

Studying the ancient trio, Rhee's racing pulse suggested the beginning of an adventure. The cleansing scent of sage overpowered the musty box, creating a veil of safety within the shop. Still, just to be careful, she raised her psychic shields before opening the letter.

Melody perched on the opposite couch, her elbows on her knees as she leaned forward. "Out loud, please?"

"Sorry. Okay." Rhee cleared her throat. "'Dear Rhiannon. Permit me to send you a gift from my store, J.W.'s Magic Emporium. I'm J.W., a collector of curiosities. I have a small storefront in Kansas City though I traveled the world to gather my gems. The three Oneiroi are statues of dream spirits.'"

"Dream spirits?"

"Sh!" Rhee said. "Save the questions. Blah, blah, okay, he says 'I knew you were the perfect recipient for my statues, after reading your website at the Institute of Parapsychology. Dream divination is a specialty of mine, as well.'"

"I told you it had to do with the Institute!"

Rhiannon paused and looked at Melody with a shake of her head. "I need to have a heart to heart with whoever put that website together. Just because I'm named for the Moon Goddess, who happens to do dream stuff, doesn't mean that's my area of expertise, you know?"

Melody bit the inside of her cheek, obviously trying not to laugh. "Uh huh."

Exhaling, Rhee went back to the letter. "'Morpheus is the leader of the trio, he holds the Dream Wand. His fierce-faced brother is Phobetor, the creator of nightmares. The third brother is Phantasos, and he imitates inanimate objects, or fantasies. Morpheus is the only one that can appear as man.' I wonder what that means?"

"No man I'd want in my dreams, thank you very much."

"I don't know," Rhiannon joked. "He'd be kind of cute if he had eyes. I love their wings."

"What else does the letter say?" Melody prodded, pointing at Phantasos.

Rhee skimmed the rest of the handwritten scrawl. She didn't have the ability to get a reading from penmanship, but she sensed that the man had a kind heart to go with his penchant for oddities.

"J.W. writes that the Oneiroi guard the dream gates, guiding the dreamer through either a saw ivory gate, or one of polished horn."

"What's the difference?"

"The ivory gate is a dream that won't come true, but the polished horn reveals the truth."

"Cool. The guarding of the dreams reminds me of the dream catchers my grandmother makes."

"Your dream catchers are pretty. The three demons? Not so much." Rhee put Morpheus next to Phobetor. Melody slid Phantasos on the other side of Morpheus. A humanesque figure, Morpheus had the build of a male, while the shorter, squat figure, covering his face with his wing as if it were a blanket, was Phantasos. The third figure, Phobetor, held its wings back in a frightening pose. The razor teeth helped. "As you said, not any guy I'd want in my dreams."

Rhee gave a giant yawn, then laughed. "Sorry. Let me finish reading this before I need a nap. Who gets up at ten on a Saturday?"

"Lots of people." Melody's eyes drooped. "I might need a second mocha."

Rhee straightened, the sense of adventure turning to apprehension as she read. "'These were sent to me anonymously a few years back. I have tried donating them to various museums, but they keep returning.'"

Suddenly, the trio took on an ominous tone. The stone seemed darker, with reddish strands throughout the beige marble. The blank eyes glimmered. Rhee shook her head, certain she'd imagined it.

"What is he saying?" Melody braided her hands together over her knee. "The museums sent the statues back?" Her knee shook.

Rhee shrugged. "I don't know. 'I've decided to close my shop and travel once more. I've already given away most of my collection. I dreamed for three nights in a row for an answer to my dilemma and Morpheus brought your name to the forefront. Please enjoy this gift. But beware! Not all dreamers can control the dream. All best, J.W.'"

"Send them back." Melody stood and handed Rhee the bubble wrap. "We'll write 'return to sender' all over the box in black sharpie."

Rhiannon reached for the moonstone pendant dangling over her sweater. "I can't send it back." Drawn to the old energy coming from the statues, she picked up Morpheus, studying the figure from every angle. Oval, blank eyes. Carved nose, wavy hair. Black wings. "He's closing the store."

"I don't like it."

Exhaling, Rhee opened her psychic net and probed for malevolence. For anything. And she got nothing. "These are just...antiques. They carry a low grade energy that isn't bad, or tainted."

"Rhee..."

Rhiannon returned Morpheus to his brothers, certain they were harmless. "I'm keeping them."

* * *

The shop door opened, and Rhiannon rose from the couch, expecting her mother. Instead, Bonnie and Corey tromped in, pink-cheeked from the cold.

"Hey," Corey said with a grin. "Your mom told us to come on back. She's making brunch."

Bonnie rolled her eyes. "And Corey said he was starving. We just ate at my house!"

"I'm a growing boy." He rubbed his stomach.

"You're lucky you're not fat."

Rhiannon interrupted their good natured bickering. "I'm glad you're here. I got something interesting in the mail."

"From who?" Bonnie asked.

Melody got up, taking the sleeping demon with her to the counter. "A strange man."

"Ooooh. An admirer?" Corey waggled his brows.

"Not that kind," Rhee said with a chuckle. "J.W. of J.W.'s Magic Emporium sent me dream demons." She joined her friends, setting the two statues down next to Melody's.

"That is freaking *awesome*," Corey sing-songed. "The only person to send me anything in the mail is my grandma – we're talking socks. You get demons. Not fair."

"They came with a warning," Melody inserted, as if someone had to be the voice of reason.

"Let me see," Corey said, practically jumping up and down.

"A warning? That's weird." Bonnie edged closer to Melody, her best friend since kindergarten.

Opposites in every way, Melody was dark, tall, and thin, while Bonnie was blonde, short and curvy. They'd always had each other's backs against Janet, who'd been a bully from the time she could hit someone over head with a rattle.

"I agree that it's odd, but come on, he's a collector. And he can't just throw away priceless antiques."

"He tried giving them away to museums," Melody tattled. "But they were returned every time. Under mysterious circumstances."

"What if he gave them to you because they're possessed or something?" Bonnie looked from the statues to Rhee.

"I think that's what he was trying to say, without saying it." Melody chewed her lower lip. "Beware!"

"Chill out guys." Rhee tapped her pendant. "I would know if they were possessed. J.W. chose me because of my name, and my supposed talent for dream divination." She touched Morpheus. "I don't feel any residual paranormal traces, just old energy."

"I think it's cool," Corey told Bonnie and Melody before turning to Rhiannon. "People in the psychic field respect your talent, Rhee, and this J.W. dude thinks you might be able to handle these statues' mojo." He slipped his arm around Bonnie's shoulders. "Are they haunted? I don't know. But Rhee is the perfect person to find out."

"Thanks, Corey. But I swear there is nothing wrong with them."

"I forget you have this whole other life. I mean, you want to be a paranormal scientist. This is what you'd do."

Bonnie blew out a frustrated breath. "When you're with us, you're just Rhee, fashionista with a ghost fetish."

Corey snickered.

"They look scary," Bonnie decided. "I don't care that they're valuable."

"Check out the fangs," Melody stage-whispered.

Corey picked up three of the stuffed kittens. "Did you peek under the fig leaf?" He practiced juggling with two, holding the third tucked beneath his chin.

"No," Rhee said, tempted to grab one of the kittens. "Pervert."

Melody covered her mouth as she yawned. "I definitely need more coffee if we're going to the movie. Corey, put those down before you ruin them. You break, you buy."

"Good store policy," Rhiannon agreed.

Corey now had all three in the air. "I got this. Watch!" One fell then he dropped the rest. "Never mind." He picked them up and put them in the basket. "Now what? Brunch?"

"We haven't had a single customer. I think the rain is keeping everyone away." Rhiannon walked around the store, straightening up, and turning off the fireplace. "Maybe we can catch a matinee."

"What about food?" Corey asked, his voice sad.

"We can eat after," Rhee said. "But if you can't wait, I'll buy you popcorn."

"I don't know where he puts it." Bonnie shook her head and shuffled toward the door.

"He's a boy." Melody stated this fact with disgust at the unfairness of his fast metabolism. "I got the keys."

Rhiannon tucked the three statues together next to the framed certificate. She couldn't wait to read up on the Oneiroi. "Let's go through the house to tell Mom we're leaving."

"And that we'll be back for brunch," Corey said.

Bonnie was first outside and she scowled up at the drizzling sky. "I'm so tired of gray and dreary weather I could scream. I want green leaves, flowers, and some sunshine might be nice too." She kicked at the cobbled pathway between Celestial Beginnings and the back of Rhiannon's house.

"I hear you. I'm ready for a change. My life is so boring it's scary." Melody reached the back door and twisted the knob. "What I wouldn't give for some excitement."

"Like what?" Rhiannon asked. "You've got school, you work here. You had a boyfriend. Maybe you should get a new one – not the delivery guy, either."

"I don't really want a boyfriend." Melody paused. "But I think my mom might have one."

"And this is the first we're hearing of it?" Rhiannon asked in disbelief. Melody's mom was pretty, and fun, and feisty too.

"She's keeping it quiet; so at first, I wasn't sure. But then I heard her giggling from her bedroom," Melody said. "You know how thin the walls are in our house."

"Did you ask her about it?" Bonnie's eyes grew wide behind her glasses.

"No." Melody walked past the washer and dryer and into the hall by the kitchen. "If she wants to tell me, she will."

"I could never hold back like that." Rhiannon spread her arms. "I can't believe you didn't fire questions at her over your morning bowl of Cheerios."

"We aren't a normal family. We don't talk about stuff. It's easier, trust me." Melody headed into the kitchen, Starla's usual place.

Rhee followed, but the kitchen was empty. "Hmm. Didn't you guys say she was downstairs?"

"She was," Bonnie said, pointing to the veggies cut on the board near the sink.

"Dad's away? A few months preggers? She's probably taking a nap."

"I could use a nap too," Melody said. "It's not like we worked that hard this morning, either, Rhee. Must be a sleepy kind of day."

"Because of the rain," Bonnie said. "I need summer."

"I'll go see. Help yourself to an apple or something."

"No thanks," Corey said, holding up his palms. "I'll hold out for popcorn."

Rhee eyed the carrot sticks. "I don't blame you." She left the kitchen, walked down the hall to the stairs and the living room. The house felt quiet. Content.

She went to her parent's bedroom on the second floor, where her dad also had an office. What used to be the guest room was going to be the baby's room. "So long as I keep the attic to myself, they can have the second floor," Rhee mumbled. "Make that the entire downstairs!"

Her mom's door was slightly ajar, and sure enough, Starla was asleep, her book open on the bed. Rhee smiled. Starla unapologetically loved romance novels. Heather

Graham, Kathleen Pickering, Cherry Adair...her 'favorite' authors were too many to list.

This one was by Patrice Wilton. Serendipity something. Shaking her head, Rhiannon decided to simply leave a note on the table downstairs and let her mom sleep. From the smile on her face, she must be having a happy dream.

She thought of Morpheus and his demonic brothers in the shop. "No nightmares, boys. You'd better make sure you give Mom the good stuff."

CHAPTER THREE

Corey drove them to the small theater in Crystal Lake's downtown. Downtown was a big park with shops on three sides. "I can't believe there's a line," he said with what could have been a whine.

"The weather's icky. What else are people supposed to do?" Bonnie stuck her hands in her jacket pockets. "I'm really bummed I lost my scarf."

"You crocheted it," Melody pointed out. "You could do another one."

"I suppose so. Can we go to the fabric store after the movie?" She smiled and hopped up and down.

"Fine with me," Corey said.

"I'm in no rush to get home," Rhiannon agreed.

"Nobody's home at my place. It gets bo-

"Boring?" Rhee, Corey, and Bonnie teased.

Melody sniffed. "Fine. Maybe I'll let Bonnie teach me how to crochet."

"It's easy. Gives you something to do besides eat." Bonnie loved to snack and was forever looking for things to do with her hands.

They each bought tickets and went inside. Rhiannon groaned. "Don't look now. There's Janet."

"With her mom." Bonnie gave Rhee a sympathetic look.

"Since Felicity is gone, Janet doesn't have anyone as mean as she is to hang out with." Melody headed toward the food counter, her prickly attitude firmly in place.

Rhiannon saw that Mrs. Roberts and Janet were seeing a different movie and sighed with relief. It didn't matter how many times she prayed for peace, something about that family set her on edge.

"Felicity might be back after spring break."

"Where'd you hear that, Corey?" Rhiannon's body immediately went from relaxed to tense. Felicity had powerful, untrained psychic abilities and she used them indiscriminately. For bad.

"Mom works with a lady who knows the family." Corey shoved his blond hair off his forehead. He needed a trim but didn't care enough to get it done. "She says Felicity really turned around and wants to come home."

"That's what all psychopaths say," Melody declared, her brown eyes hard. "She's rotten to her soul."

Felicity made Janet look like an angel. Rhee said, "School's been so much nicer with her gone. But who knows what can happen in a few weeks?"

"Yeah, like hopefully she'll slip and show her true colors at that fancy private school." Corey ordered a large popcorn, a packet of red licorice, and a giant soda. "What are you guys gonna have?"

Bonnie smacked his arm. "Some of yours."

"I want my own popcorn, thanks." Rhee ordered, getting a bottle of water too. "Corey kills his with butter."

Melody nodded and rubbed her tummy. "Just the way I like it."

The movie was just as funny as the advertisement promised – the perfect pick me up for a blah day. They'd laughed so hard Corey spilled some of his popcorn, but since it was a large, he got a free refill. When it was over, she excused herself to use the restroom. Mrs. Roberts came out just as Rhiannon went in. Face to face, they stopped inches apart, somehow managing to avoid physical contact.

They had a history, and it wasn't a good one. Janet's twin, Jared, had been Rhiannon's very first boyfriend and his family directly broke them up. Jared was nice, cute, and unfortunately, a mama's boy. Rhee was sure Janet was the devil, and Mrs. Roberts was the vessel from which they sprang. One good, the other evil.

Mrs. Roberts narrowed her eyes, refusing to move out of the way. Her mouth pursed as if she wanted to say something, or maybe she'd gotten her lips stuck to her teeth.

"Excuse me." Rhiannon moved past. Her mother said to slay them with kindness, but it was so hard.

"Rhiannon."

Caught by good manners, she had no choice but to turn around. "Yes?"

"Have you heard anything more from that man who owned the cemetery we've rebuilt?"

Rhiannon hid her annoyance at Mrs. Roberts' presumption that she'd had any influence at all over cleaning the cemetery and locating another branch of the

Roberts clan. The smart branch moved away to Seattle a hundred years ago.

"Not since he went back." She waited then asked, "Have you?"

"He called a few times, but we were too busy to chat."

I bet. Cold as ice and heartless as well. Rhiannon could imagine the runaround Mrs. Roberts gave the poor guy who just found out he had family. Rhiannon wondered if there was anything else. An uncomfortable moment passed then finally, Mrs. Roberts murmured goodbye and left.

Weird. The entire family was strange. Not in a cool way, either. Rhiannon joined her friends who waited in the warmer foyer of the theater. She didn't tell them about her encounter with Mrs. Roberts. It served no purpose and would bring a major downer to a fun afternoon.

"Let's go get some yarn! I'll make you a scarf too, Rhee, if you want one."

"Sure. Blue and silver?"

"Like I don't know your favorite colors. Please." Bonnie huffed.

"So, what are we going to do tonight?" Melody asked as they hurried to the car. The gray skies sprinkled, cooling the air.

"You guys can spend the night at my house, if you want." Rhee figured her mom wouldn't mind the company.

"Me too?"

"Nope." Rhee rolled her eyes at Corey. "She has a strict girls-only policy."

"She does not." Melody called her out. "Your mom and dad are the coolest parents on the face of the earth. Dane gets to stay at your house when he comes in from Montana to see you."

"It's a nine hour drive, not nine minutes away, like Corey."

"Don't get so defensive, I'm just saying. Your mom does not have a strict policy. On anything," Bonnie added.

"It's a special circumstance." Rhee sighed. "Fine. So what if our house doesn't have a gazillion rules. I still think asking Mom if Corey can sleep over might stretch things a bit."

"My mom would probably say no, anyway." Corey shrugged. "She's not as evolved as Rhee's parents."

"You need to be home to help her with your rotten siblings," Melody teased. "Bobby is a terror."

Rhee's phone rang and she dug it out of her jacket pocket. "Hi, Mom."

She nodded, listening to her mom yell. She covered the phone with her hand and faced her friends.

"My 'cool' mom is furious because we left the door to the shop open, and Thor got inside, knocking everything over. She says it looks like a cyclone hit it."

"But you saw me lock the door!" Melody's eyes widened. "I don't want your mom to fire me."

"She won't fire you." Rhee's heart hammered as she clearly recalled Melody closing the door with a click. "What if someone broke in?"

Rhee interrupted her mom's rant. "Mel locked the door. You better call the cops, Mom. Go inside the house! We're on our way home now."

"What? But, oh, drats." Her mom sighed. "I'll see you in a few minutes. Drive safe!"

It took ten long, scary minutes. Rhee sat on the edge of the back seat helping Corey by making sure all the lights stayed green. When they got to the house, Officer Julianne was already parked by the shop.

Rhee jumped out of the car and the others followed. "Mom? Are you okay?"

Officer Julianne, her hair dyed a bright Twizzler red, stood with her pad out, listening to Starla.

Her mom looked frightened, her blue eyes dilated as she pointed to the destruction inside the barn. "I thought the girls left the door unlocked, or open, and Thor went crazy. But one cat couldn't do all of this."

"Thor wouldn't, anyway," Rhee said in defense of her huge orange tabby.

"He was spitting at the door, tail up, fur out. I just assumed." Starla lifted a shoulder and let it fall. "I'll have to give him extra tuna later to make up for yelling at him."

Rhee put her arm around Starla's waist and hugged her, glad her mom was safe. "He'll be fine. So, what happened?"

"No broken windows, no sign of forced entry." Officer Julianne tapped her pen against the paper. "Baskets knocked off shelves, the quilts spread out, but nothing actually broken. All cash accounted for. Have you made anyone angry lately, Rhee?"

The question, posed in jest, had merit. "No. I've been an angel."

Corey snorted.

"And I know it wasn't Mrs. Roberts or Janet. They were at the movies the same time as us. Mrs. Roberts asked if I'd heard from the guy who owned the cemetery."

Officer Julianne's brow lifted. "Odd."

"Yeah." Rhee had the feeling there might have been more to the conversation but wasn't going to complain that Mrs. Roberts changed her mind.

"Well, I'll keep my ears open, but I see no real evidence here of a crime."

Starla's eyes welled, but she blinked them clear. "I suppose I should start cleaning, then."

"I'll help, Mom."

"Me too," Melody said.

"And us." Bonnie linked her arm through Corey's. "It won't take long."

"Thanks, kids." Starla turned to Officer Julianne. "Who would want to do this? I just don't understand."

"Your family has attracted a lot of attention, not all of it positive. It's part of being who you are." Officer Julianne shared a quick, sympathetic smile. "Which from what I've seen is pretty terrific. Some people are just plain jerks."

They went inside the shop, and Rhiannon's breath caught at the destructive whirlwind inside. Things tipped over or dumped out, baskets upended. "This place was spotless when we left, Mom."

"Yeah." Corey picked up one of the stuffed kittens he'd been juggling earlier. "His ear is ripped. Who would do that to a toy kitty?"

Bonnie elbowed him. "Are you sure that's not the one you dropped while attempting to juggle?" She pulled him toward the couches. "Let's get to work. We can start refolding the quilts."

Melody went to the long counter and started picking up the spilled pens and pencils, the stapler and the scissors. She liked her workspace neat and organized.

"Good thing nothing was stolen, Mom. Melody and I spent the morning putting away all that merchandise you ordered."

Starla nodded, her ever present optimism rising to the top. "It's a blessing none of those candles broke, or the vials of oils. Can you imagine the smell in here? Instant headache." She held out her hand to Officer Julianne who had followed them partway inside. "Thanks, Officer, for coming so quickly."

"I was in the area when I got the call. It's always nice to see you, although I wish the circumstances in this instance were different."

"You're welcome to come back later for tea," Starla offered. "Miles is out of town until tomorrow."

"Oh yeah," Rhee interrupted. "Mom, is it okay if Melody and Bonnie sleep over?"

"Sure!" Starla turned back to the police officer who was also becoming a family friend. "You're still invited for tea, but it might be noisy."

"I can handle noise." She put her pad away and waved as she walked to her car. "I'll call you later."

"I don't understand why this happened, but I can't do anything other than clean the mess," Starla said. "So, let's get to it."

Rhiannon smiled. Starla liked nothing better than working through a problem with her hands. "I'll pull out the ladder so we can stack the baskets."

"What's this?"

Her mom bent down, picking up the Morpheus statue from behind the tall wicker basket on the floor. She held it up for inspection.

"Oh yeah! This has been the strangest day." Rhiannon pushed her hair back from her face. "I'm so glad those weren't taken. There's two more that look like that. Brothers, called the Oneiroi."

"Greek mythology? They're dream spirits, right?"

"I guess so," Rhee said. "Anyway, these are from 200 AD, there's a certificate – oh, I see it." She went to the couch and pulled it out from under a cushion. "How on earth did it get over here? I know I put it on the counter."

Starla held Morpheus by the waist instead of the wing. "It's real?"

"Yeah." Rhiannon grinned. "Don't drop it, Mom. 200 A.D. It's so cool. Dad is gonna flip!"

"Amazing." She ran her finger over the wings. "This is in perfect condition."

"Melody doesn't like it, Mrs. Godfrey," Bonnie over-shared. "And I don't think I do either. One of them has fangs." She bared her teeth.

Starla angled the figure. "I think he's kind of cute. I love the fig leaf."

"Poor Morpheus." Rhee shook her head.

They had the store put together in less than an hour, and Starla thanked each of them with a ten-dollar bill. Rhee gave hers back with a roll of her eyes. "You can buy pizza," she said.

"I was already going to." Starla returned the ten-dollar bill to Rhiannon's pocket. "Let me give you some spending money." One of the blessings of being a paranormal prodigy was the income traveling to different events brought in. Money was not an issue, though she never took it for granted. But if her mom wanted her to have ten bucks, who was she to complain?

"Hey, Rhee, we're gonna go pick up jammies and stuff for our sleepover. Can Corey come back for movies and pizza?"

"Of course, Bon. Your boy-toy's house trained, right?" Rhee threw one of the stuffed kittens at him.

He caught it in one hand then lobbed it back. "Careful, Rhee. I might forget."

"Then you have to stay outside with Betsy and Moonstone," Starla told him with a scolding laugh.

Her friends left and Rhee was immediately drawn to Morpheus. He fascinated her. "I've got to show you the letter from J.W., who suggested doing some more reading on the dream spirits. Do you think we have any books here in the shop?"

"One, for sure, on Greek Myth," Starla said. "I'm curious too. Do you want some tea?"

"Yes, please."

Starla took two mugs from the shelf above the counter, then went to the hot water spigot and filled them. The smell of lemon zest from her tea bag wafted across the large room.

Starla carried over a tray with the mugs, a packet of shortbread cookies, and two star shaped napkins.

"Thanks, Mom."

"You got it." Starla sat down on the couch with a sigh. "Can I tell you how great it is to finally feel better?"

"You were so cute during your nap today."

"Why didn't you wake me up? The house felt so empty." She smiled with contentment. "But it won't be for long." Starla patted her barely-there baby bump. "Where did you go?"

"The movies. I left a note by the phone."

"I didn't see it."

Rhee shrugged then took a cookie while perusing the many titles Starla had in stock. "I wish I had my iPad. Amazon is bound to have a bigger selection."

"Hmm, let me see that one about Mythological Gods. And I'd like to read that letter."

"Okay. It's on the counter."

"That requires getting up. I'll take the book for now." Starla put her feet on the coffee table. "No 'thinking' it over, Rhee – just tell me what it said."

Her mom didn't like it when Rhee took telekinetic short cuts. "Fine. J.W. discovered me from the Institute."

"That's nice." Starla nibbled a cookie.

"Yeah." Rhee nodded. "So, he's closing his shop, and he's tried giving the statues to various museums, but they always come back."

"How interesting. As in, the museum returns it or a box just shows up on his doorstep? Because *that* would be strange."

"He didn't specify," Rhee said. "I have his address. He's a collector and sounds really cool. J.W.'s Magic Emporium."

Starla sipped her tea. "What a great name for a shop. It isn't easy finding the right one. Although Celestial Beginnings came to me in a dream."

"I didn't know that." Rhee pointed to the book of demi gods. "You must have passed through the polished horn dream gate."

Her mom's brow lifted.

"J.W. wrote about this, too. Morpheus and his brothers guide you, according to the myth, through the dream gate, determining what sort of dream you will have. He's supposed to be the leader of the three. We've got to find the other two." She looked around the room, her gaze settling on Morpheus.

"They have to show up somewhere, honey. Nothing else was stolen. It's awful, but I think this is a case of vandalism. We can look some more tomorrow if you want."

Rhee frowned, wondering. "Anyway," she turned back around. "The wand thing he's got is meant to direct the dreamer toward a good dream or a bad dream."

Starla put her mug down. "You have a more extensive vocabulary than referring to everything as a 'thing'."

Rhee blushed. "It's easier."

"Lazy?" Starla tapped Rhiannon's arm.

"Busted." She popped the last of the cookie into her mouth and grinned.

"I have some questions regarding the statues. What do you intuitively feel about them? Is there a reason they'd return? And where did this J.W. get them?"

"He got them from an anonymous donor. I guess he works with dreams, too." Rhee let her voice drift, wondering if that was how you passed the demons along. Special delivery, then move before the demons came back.

"Mysterious, and a little bit spooky," Starla said, her gold and silver bracelets jangling as she crossed her arms over her lap.

"The box was protected with a magickal shield. Probably to protect them from breaking, I guess. I picked up an underlying, old, energy when I touched them. Nothing negative."

"Well, you would know best with the work you've done. Have I told you today how proud I am of you?"

"Not today, no. But it's not even five o'clock yet." Rhiannon had missed her mom so much when she'd been sick that this, sharing conversation and tea, felt great.

"Funny girl." Starla took the book from Rhee. "So we have Morpheus, who comes to the dreamer looking like a regular man with a message. Then we have the brother Phobetor, who takes on the appearance of animals and monsters. He's the scary one?"

"Yep. His statue has the pointy vampire teeth."

"And they all have wings?"

"Sure do. They really are adorable."

36

"Demons are not adorable." Starla turned the page. "And brother number three, Phantasos, is sort of a dud. He can only turn into a tree, a rock, or something inanimate." She tapped the picture of Morpheus. "He's my favorite. He's the god of dream interpretation. Like your namesake. Rhiannon Selene."

"Mom, don't start." Rhee held up her hand. "I don't want to study divination. I'm happy with my courses, at school and at the institute."

"I'm just saying..."

"Let's focus on the little demons." Rhee jerked her thumb back to the counter and glanced over her shoulder.

She stilled, the hairs on her nape rising in alarm. Something off kilter, by the smallest bit. Rhee judged the distance between the cash register and where the statue stood on the counter. Closer now to the edge, wasn't it?

Frowning, Rhee wondered if she was wrong, but positive she wouldn't have scooted the statue where it was in danger of falling.

She lowered her psychic shields but felt nothing of a paranormal nature inside Celestial Beginnings.

"What's wrong?" Starla asked, putting her hand on Rhee's arm and following her gaze.

"I think the statue moved." She swallowed, her mouth dry. "By itself."

CHAPTER FOUR

"I could be wrong." Rhiannon walked over to the Morpheus statue, her psychic shields at half-mast. Partially open, to feel for psychic energy, and part closed in case she needed to protect herself in a hurry.

Starla, right behind her, said, "I doubt it. Look how near the counter it is? It's so valuable, I'm sure you would have set it in the center."

"My reasoning exactly, Mom."

"See? I can be logical." Starla smiled. "Are you scared, Rhee?"

"No." Alarmed a little, because the thing moved without her sensing anything but not frightened. The things she discovered about her gifts since moving to Crystal Lake a year and a half ago had heightened her powers. She'd also become more aware of when to use them.

Now was a perfect time to open herself up more. She reached out to touch the statue, carefully running her sensitive fingertips over the stone. Rough, ancient, a low energy hummed from the carved rock. "I'm pretty sure this is marble, but I'd like to see for sure. Certain types of stone could account for the humming I feel."

"Rocks that hum?"

WICCAN DREAM

"They have life, Mom. Same as you and me."

"I understand the basic principal, Rhee. You threw me off balance with the humming. I went to the Lord of the Rings movies and saw the talking trees."

Rhiannon snickered then focused on Morpheus. The oval eyes were clear and smooth, no pupils. Time could have erased them, though she thought not. The Greek god's hair was curly and kept close to the scalp. The staff intrigued her most. The Dream Wand.

"We're lucky your statue has a fig leaf. Most of the pictures of Morpheus, he's nude."

Rhee looked at her mother, flipping through the pages of the book on the god. "Good to know. Mom, I'm still not picking up anything mystical. I'm going to have to lower my shields to up my powers. Stand back, in case something happens."

"Are you sure that's a good idea?"

She shrugged. "I truly don't sense any harm." This bugged her, because she was almost a hundred percent certain that the statue had moved. She hadn't done it, her mom hadn't done it, and Celestial Beginnings was clear of any lingering spirits.

"Maybe there's a draft?"

Rhee rubbed her forehead. "A wind we don't feel moved a stone statue six inches across the counter?"

Sighing, Starla took a step back. "I'm ready."

Concentrating on lowering her shields, her safety net, Rhee left herself open. It was like twisting blinds, slowly letting in the light.

"Nothing." She turned and splayed her hands. "I don't get it. There should be some sort of psychic tracers from the energy used to move that statue."

"Maybe your powers are on the fritz?"

"That's ridic- can that happen?"

Starla lifted the book. "I'm just trying to be helpful. I don't know. Listen, honey, it's been a long day. Why don't we come back to this tomorrow, after a good night's sleep? We can bring the books to the house and wait for your friends there."

"But-"

Starla eyed Morpheus. "Your new friend should probably stay here."

Uneasy, Rhiannon moved the statue back to the center of the counter, marking the spot with tape. By the time they finished rinsing their mugs and tidying the shop, it hadn't budged. "I must have I imagined it." This made more sense than having her paranormal abilities not work.

They locked up, her mom pulling on the door to make sure.

"Sometimes we see things because we expect to see them."

"That makes sense in a very weird Mom way." Rhee hurried after her mom down the path to their house.

Laughing, Starla opened the back door. "Beat you!" Thor waited inside on the dryer, watching them walk in. "Thor. I'm sorry I yelled at you. Forgive me?" The orange tabby gave a slow blink, not agreeing to anything until they came to mutually acceptable terms.

"Mom said she'd give you extra tuna..."

He yowled and jumped to the floor with a loud thump. Rhee bit the inside of her cheek. "I think that means you're forgiven."

"If all problems could be solved so easily, the world would be a better place." Starla turned to the pantry and got down a can of flaky white albacore. "This reminds me. I'm hungry. For tuna fish. On crackers? With green onions." She grabbed a second can. "Just a small snack before dinner."

They went to the kitchen where Thor waited at his favorite spot over the sink. Rhee sat at the table and flipped through the pages. "There isn't that much more, just a lot of examples of Morpheus's power from Ovid."

Starla waved a knife through the air, Thor watching closely, his ears back. "I want to know about the bad brother."

"Phobetor? Sounds like a Transformer." Rhiannon laughed. "Why him, Mom?"

"So I can protect us against his nocturnal nightmares."

Rhee wasn't sure if her mom was kidding or not. She closed the book and pushed it to the center of the kitchen table. "No nightmares. J.W. didn't say anything about that, anyway. Told me to beware, something about not all dreamers being able to control the dream."

Starla arched her brow and put one hand on her hip, plastic mixing bowl in the other hand. "Maybe you should have Dr. Richards check this fellow out. See if he's heard of him."

"That's a good idea. Couldn't hurt." Rhiannon didn't want to get up, but she did want her iPad, so while her mom was dicing onions, she used telekinesis to bring it downstairs.

Thor meowed, ratting her out as the device floated into the kitchen. Starla turned just in time to see Rhee snatch it from the air. "I guess your powers are working just fine," she said in a dry tone.

"Oh yeah. I forgot about that." Rhee knew how much her mom did not approve of using her paranormal abilities all the time. She seemed to think that walking up and down the stairs was a good thing. "Which means that maybe I imagined it." She ducked her head and logged on.

"I'm not sure about that, Rhiannon."

Before she could send Dr. Richards an email, the doorbell rang.

"I'll get it," Rhee said, running out of the kitchen and down the hall to the front door.

"Don't run in the house!" Starla yelled after her.

"Sorry!" Rhee opened the door.

"Sorry already?" Melody asked, her brown eyes bright and her cheeks flushed pink.

"Mom thing," Rhee explained. Corey, Bonnie, and Mel all nodded.

"We got chips, soda, and licorice." Bonnie dropped her backpack by the coat rack then hung up her jacket. Mel and Corey did the same.

"What are you doing?" Bonnie asked, following Rhiannon to the kitchen.

"Did you get that statue thing taken care of?" Melody walked beside Bonnie.

"No. I thought I saw it move but I guess not. I taped the spot where I set it, so we can see in the morning if it moved for real."

"I like experiments!" Corey added, "When they involve explosives."

"No explosives, not even a video cam to detect spiritual activity. We're researching."

"No research, please, Rhee. It's the weekend and we should be having fun. I brought Monopoly." Corey plunked the game down at the kitchen table.

Rhee realized that just because spirits and the paranormal was her life focus didn't mean that her friends always had to be supportive. "Point received, Corey." Rhiannon set her iPad on top of the books and moved them to the side table. "Mom, do you want to play too?"

"No thank you. That game lasts forever, and I always end up in the slums. I'll cook, you guys play."

"I thought you were ordering pizza?" Rhee sat down opposite Melody, admiring her black and cobalt blue checkered sweater.

"I am. I will. Right now, I need tuna fish. Here." Starla set a tray of crackers and tuna on the table. Thor's happy purr rumbled across the kitchen as he finished his own private can.

"Cravings?" Corey nodded with understanding. "Mom ate an entire jar of dill pickles once. I kept waiting for Bobby to smell like vinegar."

Starla took another cracker and closed her eyes. "Delicious. Dill pickle would have been nice, just a touch of the juice." Her eyes flew open. "Sugar cookies. They'd be good too. Go on, go play in the living room. I have cookies to bake. And maybe a pie."

"Mom, we'll order the pizza later. No worries." Rhee herded her friends out of the kitchen.

"I love it when your mom cooks." Bonnie's ponytail brushed her shoulder.

"Did she finally give up on those muffins?" Melody, her brown hair still in braids, turned into the living room toward the long couch.

"Thank the Goddess." Rhee plopped down on the floor, legs crossed. "She's a whiz in the kitchen, but muffins evade her kitchen witch magick. Corey, can I be the boot?" She helped set out the game on the long coffee table.

Monopoly took hours, with Bonnie showing a tough streak and attempting a corporate takeover. Her mom finally ordered pizza, and Rhee ate two huge slices of extra cheese with a few sugar cookies fresh out of the oven for dessert. Before watching the B horror movie Corey picked out, she and Melody fed the animals in the barn.

Her mom, oddly a fan of fake gore, joined them for the movie. When it was over and Corey left, a contented smile on his face, Starla rose from the couch and patted her belly. "We are finally full. I didn't think it was going to happen."

"You get to eat whatever you want. That's pretty cool, Mrs. Godfrey." Bonnie gathered the dishes from the coffee table.

"This is a lot better than being sick all the time," Starla agreed. "I think Ashe has decided it's okay here."

Silently agreeing with her mom's assessment, Rhee took the dishes and garbage to the kitchen. When she returned, Starla waved from the stairs, her face sleepy. "Night, girls. Don't stay up too late. Tomorrow is supposed to be sunny for a while, and maybe you could take out Moonstone? Those poor animals have to be ready for spring too. Only a few more weeks until the Equinox."

"Sunshine in Washington State? I won't believe it until I see it." Rhiannon pointed to the stairs. "You guys ready to get into jammies? We can tell scary stories."

"No scary stories!" Bonnie's eyes flashed behind her slightly smudged lenses. "I only like the stuff that's really fake. I'll have bad dreams for sure."

"We don't want that," Rhee laughed. They'd spent the last hour and a half watching at least a hundred gallons of blood colored paint in a clown gone insane movie, but tell a ghost story? That crossed the line. "We can look at the new Teen Vogue – I've got the Spring Issue."

"Yeah." Melody's eyes glittered. "That's more like it."

"Is Dane coming down next weekend?" Bonnie asked as they reached the stairs leading to the attic and Rhee's room. "Corey likes it when he's here, so he's got another guy to hang with."

Rhee nodded. "He texted me a few times tonight. He's hoping his dad's truck route will bring him by Friday around dinner. He gets to leave school early." So far, things hadn't been that much different from when Dane had lived thirty minutes away in Tilton.

"Great," Melody said. "Then I feel like the fifth wheel." She opened Rhiannon's bedroom door and walked inside.

"No! Do you? We would never want you to feel that way." Bonnie touched Mel's back.

Mel shrugged Bonnie's hand away. "It isn't your fault. Forget I said anything. I want to hang out with you guys, but I don't want a boyfriend, so I guess I'll figure it out." She dropped her backpack by Rhee's closet. "Where's the Vogue?"

Melody's natural flare for fashion had grown a lot since getting her hands on Rhiannon's magazines. She always looked great and on a dime. "On the vanity top," Rhee said, pointing to her makeup table.

Bonnie set her backpack down by Melody's. "Mom's been great about letting me try different makeup, but she still doesn't want me wearing too much of it. I tried to do that thick black line across the top lid and it smudged everywhere."

"You have to get the liquid liner and practice," Rhee shared, picking up her own tube.

The rest of the night passed in a blur of makeup tips, boyfriend gossip, and clothes. Rhiannon fell asleep to a fashion fantasy worthy of any top model.

Too bad it was just a dream.

CHAPTER FIVE

Rhiannon bolted up at the sound of a hoarse shout, sending Thor flying from the covers as if being goosed by a ghost. Melody, conked out in a sleeping bag on the floor, awoke with a questioning shriek.

"Wake up, Bonnie!" Rhee peeked over the side of her bed at her bleary-eyed friend, the remnants of her dream disappearing. No more white Go Go boots, no more miniskirts. The sixties had been over for a while, thank the Goddess. Nancy Sinatra did not belong on Rhee's dream runway.

"What?" Bonnie asked, her eyes wide in the moonlit attic bedroom. Her sleeping bag twisted around her body and she tugged it free. "What happened?"

"You screamed," Rhiannon said, pulse finally slowing as she realized nobody was hurt.

"Are you all right?" Melody asked, looking from Bonnie to Rhiannon. "There better not be a spook in here, Rhee – you promised they were gone." Melody peeled back the sleeping bag and jumped onto Rhiannon's bed. "Scoot over."

"Make room for me too!" Bonnie dove in on the other side.

Rhiannon, now sandwiched between two of her closest friends, shook her head. "And we didn't even tell scary stories. What's wrong, Bonnie?"

"Nightmare. Yuck." Bonnie brought the covers up to her chin. "I thought I was drowning. I hate that dream."

Rhee could feel Bonnie's trembles. She was still scared, so Rhee patted Bonnie's back. "You've had this same dream before? Maybe something bad happened when you were a kid."

"I asked my mom about it once. She promised I'd never drowned." Bonnie's voice was quiet, subdued.

"Like she'd tell you," Melody laughed softly in the dark. "By the way, honey, I dropped you in the tub as a baby."

Rhee figured that was probably true. Not that it happened, but that her mother wouldn't tell her if it had.

Bonnie shivered. "I mean, I don't have it for a long time, then I forget about it, and wham – it shows up like ancient Uncle Bill with the false teeth and yellow nails, wanting a hug."

"Ew," Rhee commiserated. "Not wanted."

"I'm glad I don't have an Uncle Bill," Melody decided. "I remember you told me about this dream before, a while ago. I didn't realize you still had it."

"We can look up drowning tomorrow." Rhee added it to the research list. "I'm sure Google will have tons of stuff."

"I need one of Mel's dream catchers." Bonnie elbowed Rhee.

"Take your pick. My grandmother makes them and keeps giving them to me. What can I do? Tell her they creep me out?" She sighed and smoothed a crease in the blanket. "Mom says I have to hang them up and make Grandma happy. She doesn't care about my happiness."

Rhiannon laughed, the adrenalin from being jolted awake in the night receding in the warmth of friendship. "Your mom loves you. She loves her mom. You have to hang them." Her full-size bed wasn't comfortable sleeping three teenage girls, but it was the perfect size for sharing confidences in the dark. Besides, dawn wasn't too far off. The moon shone softly through her skylight.

"How do Wiccans get rid of bad dreams?" Bonnie asked, her eyes slowly closing as she snuggled into a pillow.

"There's probably a spell or something. We can ask Mom if she's got a favorite." She giggled low. "Rhiannon, the Moon Goddess, is supposed to be the Queen Sheba of dream interpretation. Mom reminded me earlier, when we were reading about Morpheus."

Bonnie, eyes closed, snickered. "You should probably study some, if you plan to live up to your namesake."

"I can't remember everything I read as it is. Wouldn't it be cool to have unlimited brain storage? Or at least as much as the new mini iPad." She burrowed down, her hands crossed over her stomach. Bonnie turned toward the window.

"We probably do," Melody murmured sleepily. "Once you scientists figure out how to access it all, we'll be set." She flipped toward the closet wall. "What I wouldn't give for a photographic memory."

Rhee loved the science part of her life, which used to take up most of her time. Thanks to her parent's guidance, she'd learned to merge it with the faith and magick parts too. Smiling to herself in the dark, she admitted she'd learned, kicking and screaming in protest.

"Sorry I woke you guys up." Bonnie yawned. "Tomorrow. The internet. Your mom has to have stuff as well. Or we could try the library."

"Rhiannon is practically banned from the library, thanks to that jerky librarian." Melody sniffed and sat up, raising the energy level in the room with her temper. "You could've had her fired for how she treated you. It was terrible."

Rhiannon remembered the snide comments the woman, a friend of the Roberts family, made with a knotted stomach. Though things between the Godfrey's and the Roberts calmed considerably since the cemetery incident last month, Rhee seriously doubted the two families would ever be close.

"Na. Bad karma. What I send out to the world, comes back to me times three."

"You really believe that?" Melody sounded skeptical, especially in the dark. "I mean, my dad is a total idiot. But he always lands on his feet."

"An idiot?" Rhee paused, knowing the usual rules surrounding conversation about Melody's dad. As in, not happening. "How so?"

Bonnie turned back again, facing the other two girls, her head leaning against her elbow on the pillow.

Rhee, used to her friend's angst toward her father, started to change the subject. It was off limits. Verboten. Nada.

Until the wee hours of the morning.

"He drinks. He's been in jail. Hit my mom." Melody blew out a breath. "Every bad thing you've ever heard about an Indian, 'Native American', and he's it. He is the reason for the stereotype."

Rhiannon heard the underlying shame in her friend's voice. She wasn't sure what to say, but Melody's confession explained a lot of her angry behavior.

"I'm sorry, Mel."

"I'm just saying that if there really was karma like that, he should be punished. Run over by a truck. Hit by lightning. Something that shows the universe is paying attention and does not approve. Instead, he keeps getting away with it."

"Where is he now?"

"Washington State Prison."

Wow. Not exactly getting away with it, but still, Rhiannon's heart ached for her friend. "Do you ever see him? Write him letters?"

"Are you kidding? Once Mom found out I was sending hate mail, she quit buying stamps. She seems to think Dad has reasons for being such a loser." Melody's slender hands folded together on top of the comforter. "She justifies everything he's ever done to her."

Melody had plenty of reasons for her anger. Rhee had always been curious, but the truth saddened her. She couldn't do anything to help.

"That is really crappy, Melody."

"No spell to make that go away?"

"I wish."

"Me too," Bonnie whispered.

"But," Rhiannon offered, not sure what else to do, "I can help you learn to diminish the anger in your soul, if you want."

"Why would I want that?" Melody's voice rose in surprise. "That is the only thing standing between me and the Janets of the world. My anger keeps the bullies away. My temper warns people off. I like it, Rhee. Don't mess with me."

Everybody had shields against something, and Rhiannon was in no position to tell her friend she was wrong. Until she'd learned to accept herself for being a paranormal freakazoid with Wiccan parents, she'd kept everyone at arm's length too.

She made a promise to herself that when Melody was ready to lower the wall, Rhiannon would be at her side.

Rhiannon had come to believe that the human mind was untapped of its potential, and that everyone had paranormal abilities. Which would make them all normal...something to think about on another day.

The point being, Melody had larger untapped potential, and she shut it down tighter than a bank.

Rhee wanted to help her friend open the locks and embrace all aspects of herself, but until Melody wanted the same, Rhiannon's hands were tied.

"I'm glad he's in a place where he can't hurt you." Bonnie's tones offered comfort.

"Physically, anyway." Rhee exhaled.

"Don't worry about me, kids. I am just fine." Melody lay back down, facing the wall, stiff as a board. "Nobody will get the best of me."

CHAPTER SIX

Rhiannon, Melody, and Bonnie woke up to the smell of pancakes. They followed the buttery scent down the stairs, stumbling like zombies.

"Morning!" Starla sang. Thor sat on the windowsill above the sink, looking out at the gray day, his tail twitching in time to the radio.

"Mom, can't you listen to something besides the oldies?" Rhee sank into a chair and plopped her elbows on the table.

"Why? I like the oldies. I am an oldie." She put a stack of steaming blueberry pancakes in the center. "Move your elbows, honey. Sit down, girls. Butter and syrup are on the table already. Juice? Tea?"

"Thanks, Mrs. Godfrey," Bonnie said, licking her lips. "I love blueberry."

"You love food, period," Melody teased, all signs of the predawn confessions gone. Rhee had a feeling if they brought the subject up in the light of day, her friend would deny the whole thing. "Maybe you should be a chef, Bon-Bon. You could have your own show on the travel channel. Have you seen the guy that eats all the grossest food?"

"No more talk about reality television, please." Starla humphed. "At least not first thing in the morning." She turned on the water to rinse the batter bowl.

"Mom, our Psychic Kids episode helped a lot of viewers and raised money. You have to let your anger go. Aren't you always telling me that?" Rhee slid a pancake onto her plate. Her live and let live Mom just couldn't get past the camera guy manipulating troubled kids.

"I spoke with Nathan about Jeremy and even though that terrible camera man isn't working for him anymore, there were no charges brought against him." Starla pointed her spatula at them. "I think Felicity wouldn't have gone so far if he hadn't told her what to do. Who knows what trouble he's causing now?"

Starla and Nathan had hit it off, sharing recipes, and remained in touch. The producer even offered them all a place to stay if they went to California. Maybe a sunny vacation was in order. "Getting this upset can't be good for you or Ashe," Rhee said, wanting to level out the chaotic energy in the kitchen.

At the reminder, Starla put a hand protectively over her gently rounded stomach. "I know you're right. I just don't like it." She went back to humming. "Ashe loves the oldies."

"Thanks to your influence, Mom, I actually had a dream about Nancy Sinatra and those white boots she wore on one of her album covers."

Starla turned and smiled. "You should look the video up on YouTube. It does my heart good to know that some of my culture has rubbed off on you."

Bonnie and Melody laughed, helping themselves to breakfast. "I guess we all had weird dreams," Bonnie said. "Maybe it was the sugar cookies?"

"Never!" Starla denied. "Eat your pancakes, girls."

Rhee took a bite, letting the sweet-tart combination of the blueberry settle over her tongue. The best miracle in the world was having her mom happy, healthy, and cooking again. Her baby brother, barely more than an amoeba, had psychically connected with her, promising to stick around.

All her mom wanted to be, ever, was a mom.

Rhiannon couldn't imagine living life with such a focused view but figured Bonnie probably could. Bonnie wanted to live in Crystal Lake, marry Corey, work at the casino, and have a family. Simple but true blue. Rhee wanted the world.

"I had to call your dad. It rained all night, and a corner of the barn is leaking. He has plans to stop at the hardware store on the way home from the airport and buy supplies to fix it."

Giggling, Rhee looked at her mom. "Really? Do you have 911 on speed dial?"

"Yes. Yes I do." She took a drink from a mug that read "Kitchen Witch."

"Why speed dial?" Melody asked.

"Fair question." Rhee put her fork down and reached for her juice. "Every time he tries home improvement, he needs stitches —well, that one time he only sprained his ankle. That wasn't too bad."

"And then he had to call the handyman, anyway." Starla shook her head and sighed. "It would be easier for him to start with the handyman, but he refuses. Stubborn."

"Is that where you get it?" Melody clinked her butter knife against Rhee's plate.

"Me? Stubborn? I have no idea what you are talking about." Rhiannon changed the subject before they all came up with legit examples of her behavior. "Hey Mom, do you know anything about drowning in a dream?"

Starla turned down the radio and sat at the table. "Hmm. Interesting. Are you drowning?"

"Not me. Bonnie."

Starla pushed a lock of red hair, similar in shade to Rhee's, behind her ear. "Dream interpretation enthusiasts have different ideas about the meanings of things. Freud and Jung each had theories about-"

"Who?" Bonnie asked, her eyes narrowing in concentration.

"Sigmund Freud and Carl Jung. Psychologists at the turn of the century who delved extensively into dream research."

"We need something current, Mom." Rhiannon tossed a blueberry across the table. "I think we've come a long way since the couch."

"Okay, smarty pants, you asked me, remember?" Starla popped the blueberry into her mouth and chewed. "It's supposed to be a magical skill of the moon goddess. But anyone can do it. Don't be afraid to tap into your center."

Rhee nodded, accepting that her mom just spoke like that, and grateful she had friends who accepted it. It hadn't always been that way.

"I told her she should study." Bonnie stood, picking up their empty plates. "What do you think about dream catchers?"

"They're said to catch the bad spirit causing a bad dream in the net, while allowing the good spirit-dreams through. You should hang it over your bed. Specifically, your pillow." Starla rose and walked to the sink, turning on the water and accidentally splashing the cat.

"Woops," Rhee said. "One of the dangers of sitting so close to the sink."

Thor flattened his ears and leaped to the floor, complaining the entire way out of the kitchen.

"I always thought dream catchers were pretty and wanted to learn to make them." Starla stacked the dirty dishes to one side of the sink.

"Melody's grandma could teach you," Bonnie said.

"She knows how?"

"Yeah," Melody admitted. "She used to sell them but it isn't as popular anymore."

"I'd like to see one! I wonder if we should carry them in the store?" Starla looked at Melody, who blushed.

"I could ask."

"No big deal, honey. But if she is interested, I'd be happy to talk to her." Starla squirted organic dish soap into the sink.

"Want me to wash, Mom?" Rhiannon put the juice in the refrigerator.

"Nope. I got this. You girls enjoy the morning." She leaned over and looked at the clock. "Feed the animals? Moonstone and Betsy could use a romp in the fresh air."

It didn't take them long to get dressed and head outside. The trek to the barn out back of the house took five minutes. Moonstone neighed, Betsy snorted. Thor, dry once more, leaped to the top of the feed bin. Rhee could see where the barn had leaked, opposite the end of the pet's stables.

She probed for negative energy, but the air was clear. "Probably too cold for ghosts," Rhee muttered.

"If that was the case, you wouldn't have been able to free that little girl's spirit in the cemetery," Bonnie said.

"True. I still think it's weird how Psychic Kids uncovered Crystal Lake's murky beginnings. How Mom and Dad thought they were bringing me someplace without a single psychic blip, but instead, it's a hot bed of paranormal activity."

"You were meant to come here and be our friend," Bonnie declared with a grin. "Bring some excitement to this old dairy town."

"Finding a forgotten gravesite," Melody lifted a finger, then another. "And the dead body in the lake."

"Solving the mystery of the fake diamonds," Bonnie added in a rush.

"Crystal Lake probably put out some mojo, which your mom picked up on, knowing that you could uncover the secrets and make our town a better place to be." Melody braided her long, dark hair into a single plait, deftly tying it with a black scrunchie, then topped her 'do with a knit cap.

"I'd never seen a ghost in my life." Rhee laughed self-consciously as she remembered her introduction to Crystal Lake. "Fourteen and mad about the move. I was so scared when I saw it I fainted in the front yard. I mean, then Mom wanted me to stay in the same room I saw the face in the window?"

"No wonder you fainted. I would have cried." Bonnie held out her hand for Betsy to nuzzle before scratching behind the gorgeous cow's ears.

Rhiannon ran her finger down Moonstone's nose, the velvet skin soft and warm. The horse blew out a breath and Rhee laughed. "You want to play? Are you tired of winter too?"

Her tail swished back and forth and she stomped her front hoof.

"I think that's a yes." Melody opened that stall gate.

"Can Betsy come? It's only fair," Bonnie said, already undoing to the latch.

"Sure! We can take them to the corral and give them some hay. Let them enjoy the brief show of sun."

"Are you going to ride her?" Melody asked, pointing to Rhiannon's saddle.

"Maybe later. I'm dying to figure out what Bonnie's dreams mean. Oh and we couldn't find two of those statues. We have Morpheus but not his brothers. I want to search the shop again. Nothing else was taken, so they've got to be misplaced."

"And we have to see if Morpheus moved from the taped spot," Melody reminded her. "I hope it is exactly where you left it."

"Even if it is possessed or haunted or whatever, it's still a very valuable item. Maybe I can just bless it and it will be fine."

"The guy that sent it to you?" Bonnie shivered. "I bet he's probably thinking good riddance."

"It's not that bad." Rhiannon doubted she'd seen anything at all.

They stepped out into the crisp spring morning, their breath clouding before them. Moonstone pranced and took off at a run. Could winter finally be done?

"Guess someone is happy to be outside." Rhee patted Betsy's solid warmth. "Go on, girl. Kick up your heels." The cow gave her a look as if to ask who Rhee was speaking to. Kicking was not in her repertoire. Laughing, Rhee kissed Betsy's nose. "Not you, then."

Betsy ambled at a sedate pace across the fenced in, grassy area, her ears twitching.

"Pets with personality." Melody crossed her arms, looking adorable with her bangs side swept above her brows. "Mom says no pets for us. We can barely take care of ourselves."

"You can borrow our dogs any time you want," Bonnie offered. "Four is ridiculous, and all those mutts do is lick, lick, and shed. And occasionally bark at stuff nobody else can see."

"Animals sense ghosts," Rhee said. "It's been documented a million times."

"Are we surprised?" Melody shook her head. "I'm just not crazy about the idea of a bunch of invisible stalkers. I could reach out my hand and touch somebody? Yuck." She took off after Moonstone, who was in the mood for tag.

After an hour or so, Rhee put her hand to her cheeks. "I can't feel my face anymore. I'm frozen to the core."

Bonnie nodded, her lips having a bluish tint. "I didn't want to be the first to complain, but I'm freezing."

"Hot chocolate?" Melody's eyes sparkled. "In front of the fireplace?"

"We can have Celestial Beginnings to ourselves." Rhee rubbed her hands together. "Let's go."

The three girls tromped across the small field between the barn and the shop. They reached the door, and Melody tried to open it. "Locked."

Not wanting to run back to the house, Rhee lifted her brow and telepathically unlocked the door.

"Cool trick," Bonnie said with a giggle. Melody rolled her eyes.

They went inside, and Rhiannon flicked on the lights, illuminating the dark and banishing shadows.

"Good morning, Celestial Beginnings." Melody took a deep breath and smiled a rare, genuine, Melody smile. "Cinnamon, orange. Rosemary. I love it here."

"Me too," Bonnie said. Familiar with the layout, she headed toward the hot water spigot and retrieved three mugs. "Hot chocolate?"

Rhiannon nodded, watching Mel and Bonnie with a spurt of gratitude. Since Rhee traveled back and forth to the Institute of Parapsychology, it wasn't always feasible for her to help her mother. Starla hired Melody, a few hours here and there, and sometimes got Bonnie for free. Her friends were the best.

Melody turned on the electrical fireplace. It gave warmth, but mostly created mood. Her gaze went to the long counter where Bonnie was setting out the mugs.

There was the tape. Where was Morpheus?

CHAPTER SEVEN

"I swear, I put that statue right there, X marks the spot." Rhee, hand on her hip, searched the counter. The floor. Table. Nothing. "Did you touch it, Bonnie?"

"Are you kidding?" She shivered.

Melody walked over to stare at the taped counter, then took her hat off and dropped it on the table. "So where is it?"

"Maybe Mom moved it earlier." Rhee could tell the missing statue really freaked out both her friends, and deliberately sent out a wave of calm.

"You could call her." Bonnie put three steaming mugs on a tray and walked around the counter to the couches and table. "The certificate is by the cash register."

Rhiannon went over and looked; the framed document was lying right where she'd left it yesterday. "It's no big deal." Where was it? Was it with the other two statues? She could ask her mom, but she had a good idea what the answer would be, and she didn't want to scare her friends with a wandering foot tall marble demon. Especially when she was beginning to think it would show up when it felt like it, and not until then.

As if Morpheus was playing a trick.

Taking a deep, centering breath, she walked to the shelves of books. "Mom and I took the mythological gods one to the house, but there are a lot more on basic dreaming and interpretation."

The girls each took a seat. Melody and Bonnie held a mug and sniffed.

"Mmm." Bonnie sighed appreciatively. "This is ten times better than a tree house."

"What?" Melody asked in surprise. "Totally not following that train of thought."

Embarrassed, Bonnie quickly explained. "I mean, I always wanted a clubhouse or someplace to go that was mine. With friends. Remember a couple summers ago, Mel, when all the boys were building tree houses?"

Melody scrunched her nose and nodded. "I guess."

"I used to put blankets over my bed and pretend but it wasn't the same." Bonnie sighed.

"I'm by myself all the time. I don't need a place like that. But this," Mel gestured with her mug, encompassing the entire room. "This is cool."

"Mrs. Edwards says it is the relationships we form that matter most in this life." Rhiannon blushed, regretting the adult sounding opinion as soon as the words left her mouth.

"She's the Irish lady from the Institute, right?" Bonnie asked. "She seems really nice."

"She's very talented, too, and a world renowned medium. Someday, maybe I'll go that route. But I like the nuts and bolts of the brain too much to give up the science aspect for good."

"What's the difference between a psychic and a medium?" Bonnie sat on the edge of the couch. "Is it the same?"

Rhee could tell that Melody was curious, though she'd never admit it. "A medium specifically connects with the dead. Psychics are intuitive people who utilize their sixth sense. All humans have the ability to some degree."

"Even me?" Bonnie sat back and put her hand to her chest.

"They are still studying-"

"Okay, Dr. Godfrey," Melody said in a teasing voice laced with sarcasm, the defensive kind, Rhee noted. "Let's get back to Bonnie's dream."

"Someday, Mel, someday." Melody had her reasons for being prickly, but there would come a time when the defenses would lower. Like last night. Rhee opened the book in her lap. She slid her finger down the page, pausing at sentences of interest. "Wow. There are a lot of scenarios. Are you drowning alone? It means you feel overwhelmed. Is someone with you? Do you love that person – hate them?"

"I'm alone. I mean, I don't remember it clearly, just the feeling of it. Being scared, unable to breathe."

Rhee read further. "Here, it has being drowned by someone, on purpose." She looked up. "Is someone hurting you?"

Bonnie set her mug down with a clatter. "That would be terrible. No, no, it isn't like that."

"Listen, I have a million dream catchers. Come pick one out. My mother won't even notice, I promise."

"Isn't that bad juju or something?" Bonnie's nose wrinkled.

"How could it be? I don't think I dream at all, actually. And my grandmother made them. Filled with love." She grinned, twisting the tip of her braid.

"So what's the difference between your grandma's mojo and tapping into your own psychic ability?" Rhee asked pointedly.

At first, Rhee wasn't sure Melody would answer but she did. "Grandma chooses to use it. I don't want to know. I don't think seeing ghosts or spirits sounds like fun. I've watched you, I've seen Grandma, and I believe there is a perfectly good reason for a veil between the dead and living."

Rhee's mouth dropped open. She snapped it closed. "I understand, Melody. I won't bug you about it anymore."

Bonnie studied Melody then nudged her best friend. "Sounds perfectly logical to me. Honestly, now that I've had that dumb dream, it could be months before I have it again. We can do something else if you want."

Thor, who had followed the girls into the shop, let out a distinctive meow. He leaped down from the highest shelves, curling up on the couch by Rhee.

Curious as to what she had in her hand, he stuck his nose in the mug then retreated with his ears back.

The girls laughed. "I guess he doesn't like peppermint," Rhee said, smoothing her hand down his thick, soft fur.

"What's the worst dream you ever had?" Melody asked Rhiannon.

Bonnie peered over her glasses. "I'm sure it was scary."

Shrugging, Rhiannon thought back to the time she'd been possessed by Suzanne, and to Matthew, one of her best friends who lived in Las Vegas, who had terrible things happen as he slept. "Remember Matthew's repressed memories? Those were awful. He started fires."

Bonnie shivered. "Poor Matthew. I felt terrible for him, and to have his uncle trying to kill him? It turned out for the best and now he's a gazillionaire, but how is he feeling? Are he and Tanya still dating?"

Rhee sighed heavily. "It's not that we aren't close friends, we are, but it's different when you live together, as we all did at the Institute. Now, we Skype and text but you miss the little things."

"Well?" Melody prodded. "Are they still dating?"

"Yeeees. But they're just sixteen, well, Matthew's seventeen, but they're young. Who knows where life will take them?"

Bonnie's eyes shut briefly. When she opened them again, they were a fierce blue. "Just because you are young when you fall in love doesn't mean it won't last."

Rhee knew Bonnie was thinking of Corey. "Some people marry their childhood sweethearts and it does last forever." She nodded. "Look at Bon Jovi."

"Not very often," Melody rebutted.

"My mom and dad have been married for almost twenty years. There's been a few bumps, but they still love each other." Rhee remembered how she'd worried over them getting divorced, and now there was a baby on the way. A very psychic baby.

"Mine? Not so much." Mel dropped the book she'd been half-heartedly looking at on the couch. "Mom married my sperm donor,"

"Melody!" Bonnie choked out.

"Dad." Melody corrected with narrowed brown eyes. "They got married because of me and divorced because of me. I wish Mom would have saved us the trouble by not saying 'I do.'"

Rhiannon winced at the underlying pain in Melody's voice and decided to change the subject. "Listen." She tapped the book. "Dreams of drowning seem to imply a feeling of no control, of being out of control. Have you been feeling that way?"

"You used to be super shy," Melody said, going along with the switch in topics. "But you're a lot better. It seems like you wouldn't have the dream now you're more secure."

"Is there something going on that, well, seems threatening to you?"

Bonnie chewed her thumbnail. "I worry, sometimes, that Corey and I will break up. That he'll realize I'm not the prettiest girl, or the coolest, or..." She looked down into her mug, as if she could find answers in the dregs of cocoa.

Melody slipped her arm around Bonnie's shoulders. "You are the best. Corey knows it."

Rhiannon tilted her head. "Instead of a spell to ward off bad dreams, I think we need to give you a confidence booster. What if your dream of drowning is a warning to stay confidant in yourself? Don't buy into the media hype. Beauty comes in all forms and most of it is in here."

Rhee tapped her chest. "A confidant woman can pull off wearing a Hefty bag."

Bonnie giggled. "I don't think so."

Melody sat back and grinned. "Remember my fairy costume?"

"I thought it was beautiful." And daring and fun. And it had the added advantage of bugging Janet Roberts. Of course, that had ended with disastrous consequences...Rhee focused on the present.

Rhiannon got up and went to an old, slim volume of witchcraft. "How about this spell, Bon?" She opened the fragile catalogue and read, "Eye of newt, tongue of fruit bat, tail of a two headed glass snake." Rhee held the precious document to her heart. "I love this."

"Weird." Bonnie shook her head. "I know you're teasing, but I still think it's weird."

"Something more modern?" Rhee chose a book with herbs and broomsticks down the spine and cracked it open.

"What's it say? I don't want to do anything, well, scary."

"Like an animal sacrifice?" Rhiannon asked with a straight expression.

Bonnie's face paled. "No, oh no."

"Wiccans don't do that," Melody said, shaking her head. "Rhee's teasing you."

"We're vegetarians, Bonnie. We don't kill to eat, we don't kill for a sacrifice."

"I know." Bonnie pressed one hand to her stomach and with the other, grabbed the book. "Let's see this."

She read, humming, then looked up with a smile. "Here's one!"

"What is it?" Melody asked, trying to read over Bonnie's shoulder.

"A confidence spell." She hummed some more, then summarized. "I should do it in the morning, so the spell lasts all day. Just takes a few minutes."

"What do you need?" Rhee asked.

"Is it easy?"

Bonnie nodded, her expression serious. "Yes, it's easy, Mel. I can't believe I'm going to do this." She looked up at Rhiannon. "I would love to be more confident. This says I need a piece of rose quartz."

"Sure." Rhee knew that was for love, not just receiving love but to love yourself too.

"A mirror." Bonnie's lip curled. "And a natural fiber pouch. It suggests cotton or silk."

"All easy enough to find. What next?"

"Rhee, you might have to help me with this part. It says I have to cleanse the stone, to get rid of other unwanted energy."

"You do that in your room, when you burn sage, right?" Mel asked.

"Yeah. Does it say, Bon, how they want you to do it?"

"There are options." Bonnie giggled nervously. "Bury it in a bowl of sea salt for a full day and night, or leave it in sunlight, or in the light of the full moon for a whole night. Oh here, Rhiannon, she suggests smudging too. White sage or cedar!"

Rhiannon lifted a brow. "White cedar? I bet that smells good."

"It says to hold the stone in the smoke, to make it ready to receive my energies."

"Who wrote this again?" Rhee asked.

"Twyla DiGangi, and she gave credit to Simon Lilly and a book called Crystals and Crystal Healing." Bonnie read directly from the copyright page.

"If the spell works," Mel said, "you should write her."

"Really?" Bonnie perked up. "That would be awesome. Do you think she'd mind?"

Rhiannon smiled, thinking of the personal notes people sometimes sent to her. Just knowing that someone took the time to write felt as good as a hug. "She would love it. What's the rest?" Rhee asked.

"Cleanse the mirror with cold running water. As the water goes down the drain, imagine negativity washing away too. I'm paraphrasing, of course."

"Of course," Rhee parroted with a suppressed laugh.

Bonnie ran her finger down the page. "She says we can add a sprig of white sage or cedar to the pouch to keep my mirror free of unwanted energy." She squirmed as she read more then looked up, worry in her eyes. "I don't know guys, is this too weird?"

Melody took the book and read in a commentator's voice. "Perform Mirror Magick to Build Self-Esteem Spell."

She cleared her throat. "The first morning, get your tools together. Find a quiet, comfortable place to sit. Hold the rose quartz in one hand and the mirror in the other. Gaze into the mirror and say: "Oh gracious Goddess / Who gave me life / Help me to see / My beautiful side."

"That's nice," Rhee said.

"Keep gazing into the mirror and begin to contemplate all of your good qualities and abilities. Tell yourself how beautiful you are, how caring and kind, thoughtful, and lovely, and whatever else is good and positive. Many will begin to "feel" a sensation working inside; the experience tends to be a bit different for everyone, but it could feel warm or tingly. Once you feel that sensation, sit for a few minutes and really absorb it. It's believed that the sensation is a sign that is the spell starting to cloak you." Melody stopped reading.

"Will it hurt?" Bonnie asked.

"No, Bon," Rhee said. "I promise."

"After, thank the Goddess for aiding you," Melody read. "Carefully place the mirror in its pouch and store it somewhere it will be safe. Keep the rose quartz on you, stored in a pocket or purse. Do this spell each morning. It won't be long before you begin to feel all the good things you tell yourself every morning. Do your best not to allow negative thoughts into your mind during the day. If you find yourself doing that, stop and take a deep breath. Think back to the morning ritual and reaffirm all the positive things you told yourself until the negative thoughts disappear."

Melody looked up. "This is all good stuff, Bonnie. Here's the rest. 'You may feel a little silly the first few times you perform this spell. That is normal, just keep with it, and don't try to be modest. Keep in mind that mirror magick is very powerful magick. It is reflective magick and a pathway to your soul. Whatever you tell your reflection is reflected back on to you and your soul, allowing you to heal. Never tell the mirror negative things as it will come back on you quickly and powerfully.'" Melody lowered the book. "This actually sounds amazingly cool."

"Really?" Bonnie asked, uncertain.

"We have rose quartz and those cute mirrors that came in Friday's shipment. We'll have to find a pouch," Melody said decisively.

"Do you think you can do this, Bonnie? It seems simple but good. I think it's a good fit for you." Rhee plopped down on the couch, scratching behind Thor's ears.

"It does sound silly, talking to myself like that." Bonnie took a deep breath. "But if it helps keep that dumb dream away, I'll try it." The door opened and the girls jumped back.

"Rhiannon, you have a visitor." Starla walked into the shop, followed by a green-eyed blonde with a permanent sneer.

"Janet?" Melody asked in a disbelieving voice.

Rhiannon sighed – her amazing day had just taken a drastic turn for the worse. Their "tree house" had been invaded by the enemy.

CHAPTER EIGHT

"What are you doing here?" Rhiannon asked, staying in her relaxed pose on the couch.

"Rhiannon!"

"Sorry, Mom." Rhee put her book down and motioned for Bonnie to do the same. Bonnie's cheeks were pink, as if she'd been caught doing something wrong. She had to keep Janet's attention on herself until Bonnie got it together or Bonnie would become a target.

"Hi, Janet." She felt her mom's warning glance. Be nice, be nice. She could practically hear her mom's thoughts. *I can't.* "What are *you* doing here?"

Janet sashayed into the room as if she owned the place. Or thought she could at least buy them out. "It's okay, Mrs. Godfrey. Why should Rhiannon pretend to like me?"

Starla held her hands at her waist, fingers interlaced. Her mouth thinned, but she didn't answer Janet's rhetorical question.

Rhee stood, dumping Thor to the ground. "Janet, can I help you with something? You really should have called." Instead of invading their space. Maybe she'd try some of Twyla's white cedar to cleanse it once Janet left.

"And have you ignore the phone?" Janet shook her finger.

Melody came to stand beside Rhee, and Bonnie, calmer now, took her other side.

Starla hovered at the door, looking at Rhee. *Stay, go? Go. Thanks.*

Starla lifted her hand in a frustrated wave and shut the door, trapping the four girls in the room together.

"Now that your mommy's gone," Janet said, shrugging out of her coat and slinging it over her shoulder. "I'd like to issue an invitation. Private." She flicked a cool gaze over Melody and Bonnie. "For Rhiannon, only."

"I'm sure I'm not interested." Rhee stayed with Mel and Bonnie.

Janet winced. "Ouch." She took a deep breath. "Have it your way. As much as it pains me, I come on behalf of the riding team. With Felicity gone, there is a spot open. You showed potential last year. Trust me when I say there is nobody else to ask. If you don't join, the team won't be able to compete. Crystal Lake has always competed."

"And you always win. I remember." Rhee took a single step toward Janet. "I can't help you. I didn't like it." She knew how much it must've sucked for Janet to come and ask for help. As much as she would like to add 'ha ha' to the rejection, her belief in good over evil wouldn't allow it. "You really can't find anyone?"

"We have two young riders, inexperienced. If we can get to the qualifications, then maybe I could work with them, but right now, they suck."

"Nice." Melody rolled her eyes.

74

"I wasn't speaking to you," Janet snapped.

Rhee took a moment to absorb the information. "What does it mean to qualify?"

Janet's shoulders relaxed a half inch. No more. "Three riders have to time at a minimum of ten seconds. Right now, we have me. Sandy broke her leg Thursday, and Felicity's gone, leaving me novices who are mostly afraid of their horses."

The last thing Rhiannon wanted to do was spend any one on one time with Janet Roberts. Her free time was precious, and to be around someone like her? Her negative energy would add instant wrinkles. "We still have the bucking machine. You are welcome to use it."

Janet gave a short, clipped nod. "That's great. I need you ready by next weekend."

"Whoa!" Rhee held out her arms, looking at Bonnie and Mel. Did Janet not listen or what? "I told you I don't want to. You can use the electronic bull to get your novices ready."

"In a week? That won't happen. If you could join, help us qualify, then just stay on the roster, you won't have to ride once we get the other girls trained."

"Don't you get it? She said no." Melody, hands clenched, crowded next to Rhiannon.

Janet gritted her teeth, her eyes narrowing but knowing she had to be very careful. Making Rhee mad wasn't in her best interests.

"Why should Rhiannon help you?" Bonnie asked, pushing her glasses up the bridge of her nose. "You've been awful to her since she moved here."

"She isn't scared of you, you can't bully her. You have no power over her." Melody laughed low. "So why should she do anything for you?"

Anger splotched Janet's tanned face. "It's not for me, it's for the school. Crystal Lake has always held the championship."

"Maybe it's time for another school to have a shot." Rhee shrugged. "I am not saying no to be mean. I just didn't like riding like that."

"You're afraid." Janet stared, her eyes green, hard chips.

"No." Rhee frowned. Did Janet not understand the meaning of the word *no*?

"What if Jared agreed to train with you?"

Rhee sucked in a breath, surprised Janet thought that might sway her. "Really? That is so over. Thanks though. You know where the door is." She couldn't believe Janet had the nerve to dangle Jared like a tempting carrot. As if!

Janet stomped her foot. "Listen, Rhiannon, this is a Crystal Lake tradition."

"I am not from Crystal Lake."

"No kidding. You've managed to come here and disrupt everything. And when asked for one simple favor, you say no."

Rhee's temper, which she'd worked so hard on controlling, spiked. She saw the Home Sweet Home hanging sway and tamped her anger down. "As my friends said, I don't owe you anything."

"I knew Jared was wrong. He seems to think there's some good in you, but I told him he was crazy."

Jared suggested Janet ask Rhee? That was the crazy part. Jared was the complete opposite of his evil sister. He was kind, thoughtful, and out of his mind, if he thought she would do a single thing for Janet.

"Guess so." Rhee crossed her arms and looked longingly toward the door. If Janet wouldn't leave, maybe she, Bon, and Mel could escape? Janet moved a little, and Rhee froze.

The Phobetor statue gleamed from the corner nearest the front door, wings lifted, fangs glistening.

How had it gotten there? Her neck chilled with awareness. Had her psychic display of emotion energized the statues?

Janet snapped her fingers. "Earth to Rhee! Jared said to tell you that the school that wins provides four memberships to underprivileged kids for summer camp."

Jared knew how to play dirty. Dane might even approve. The statue seemed to blink in the shadow.

Eerie.

She had to get her friends, and even Janet, out of the shop. Now. "I'll call you later."

"What?" Bonnie and Mel asked in unison, stepping forward.

"You will?" Janet grabbed Rhiannon's arm.

Rhee was the only one facing the door. The statue winked – an impossible trick of the light since it only had smooth, lidless orbs.

She shook herself free. "Yeah. You better go, now, before I change my mind."

Melody sniffed, not quite believing her ears. She walked back to the couch. Bonnie wavered, as if uncertain. Follow Mel or protect Rhee?

"It's okay, Bon." Rhee pointed to the door. "Janet's leaving."

Janet, offended, allowed herself to be herded toward the door.

Rhee prayed with all her might that the statue would stay hidden in the corner.

She wondered why she wasn't picking up any psychic ability, concluding that the entity had a powerful shield. How? Who? Rhee needed answers now that she had proof it was really possessed. Preferably before Janet noticed, or her friends, that the demon could move.

Janet and her riding problem was the least of Rhee's worries. She'd figure out the details later.

"Don't forget." Janet stopped short almost at the threshold. "We have to qualify Saturday."

"Dane will be here," Bonnie reminded Rhee.

Rhiannon paused, not wanting to give up any time with Dane when he'd traveled from Montana just to see her.

"It won't take long. A few hours. You'll be back home by noon." Janet seemed desperate, almost as desperate as Rhiannon to get her out of the shop. She lowered her voice. "Please, Rhiannon."

The fanged statue inched forward with a barely audible scraping sound, but it caught Janet's attention, and she turned to see what was behind her.

Rhee coughed, taking Janet by the elbow and moving her closer to the exit.

"Thanks. We can talk at school tomorrow." She realized Janet's dangling scarf was precariously close to the floor. She watched as if invisible fingers tugged on the end. Slowly. Imperceptible, if you weren't looking for it.

"I get it! I'm leaving, you don't have to push." Janet pulled her elbow free of Rhee's hold and opened the door, the scarf going beneath it as she went one way and Phobetor yanked the other.

Janet fell back into the doorframe with a yip, glaring at Rhee. Rhiannon quickly held up both hands. "What?"

"I don't like you," Janet breathed out.

"I know."

"Just so we are clear. Don't expect to be best friends once this is over."

"You need me, remember?"

"It makes me sick to my stomach. But yeah, I got it."

She pulled her scarf free of the door and walked out, head held princess high.

Rhee slammed the door behind her, glaring at the statue, which was once again flush against the wall, as if nothing happened. It made her doubt her own eyes.

But she knew better.

CHAPTER NINE

"I can't believe you agreed to help her." Melody shook her head as Rhee turned toward where her friends stood by the couch. Baskets and displays blocked their view of the floor near the front door. They had no idea Phobetor was there.

"I know you want to help those kids, Rhee, but is it worth being around Janet?" Bonnie's voice exuded worry. "She's so negative. Nasty. Blah." She stuck out her tongue as if the air tasted icky.

"Talk about bad mojo. I'm not surprised she doesn't have any friends left. Who wants to put up with that? Where's the karma thing with her, huh?"

"Melody, Janet has friends. Remember Mutt and Jeff? She can't be a complete jerk all the time." Rhee shrugged, trying not to show her concern. "Let's go back to the house and see if we can find a pouch for Bonnie's mirror and rose quartz. I'll copy the spell for you. We have a printer in Dad's office."

She wanted them out of Celestial Beginnings and away from the statues. She wasn't sure what was happening, but the fact that it yanked Janet's scarf without Rhiannon picking up a hint of psychical energy meant they were very, very strong.

And tricky. Were the brothers pranksters?

The girls grabbed their coats and closed the shop. Rhee wasn't at all surprised to see Phobetor had disappeared again. *I'll be back. When Dad gets home, watch out.*

Murmuring a blessing of protection over the store, Rhiannon locked up, and the girls tromped across the path to the house. She led the way inside, taking a deep sniff of apple spice. Pie. "Mom, are you trying to make us all fat?"

Starla, flour dotting her nose, wiped her hands on her apron. "What did Janet want? I was about ready to come over there with my rolling pin. I've been dying of curiosity."

"She needs me to fill in on the riding team. One of the girls broke her leg, and Felicity moved. She needs five, and the three other girls are novice freshman."

"That took guts. What did you say?" Starla asked with surprise.

"She started off with no," Melody shared.

Starla crossed her arms. "And then?"

"If we win, and chances are good with Janet's skills, it buys summer camp registrations for kids who wouldn't be able to go otherwise."

"Ah. She got to your heart strings." Starla pursed her lips and nodded.

"I'm a sucker. Jared told Janet to tell me that – he's the one who knew."

"Because he's the one Roberts family member who knows what a heart is," Melody declared.

"I still can't believe you agreed." Bonnie shook her head and helped herself to a glass of water. "Mrs. Godfrey, I owe you for a mirror and piece of rose quartz from your store."

Starla grinned. "A self-confidence spell? I like that one. Reinforces our inner beauty. And honey, you've helped out plenty at the store for nothing. Take that as trade."

"Really?" Bonnie smiled. "Thank you."

"I'm going to copy the words for her. Uh, Mom, do you have a pouch? You could show me," Rhee said, thinking, *Come upstairs with me.*

Starla frowned.

Rhee didn't even want to know what her mother thought she heard. She grabbed Starla's hand. "Come with me." She looked at her friends. "We'll be right back."

"What's the rush?" Starla asked, cheeks flushed. "Did you ask about a hairless monkey?"

"I really hope you and Ashe have better communication than you and I do."

"Do you think we might?" Starla placed her hand against her stomach. "I haven't heard a thing."

"I think he's sleeping. I haven't heard him, other than a soul vibration, since he decided to stick around."

"But he's still there?" Starla's voice trembled.

Rhee, realizing how scared her mom was, gave her a quick hug. "Yeah, he promised. He's growing. Takes a lot of work."

"Okay." Starla exhaled and turned on the printer. "Let me copy that spell. What did you want to talk to me about away from the girls?"

"Phobetor. Morpheus."

"The statues or the demi gods?"

"The statues. Phobetor is possessed for sure. It tried to choke Janet when she left the store. Tugged on her scarf. Somehow. I couldn't see because the statue was on one side and I was with Janet on the other."

Her mom's face paled, leaving a few freckles along her nose. "Was she hurt? The last thing I want to deal with is a phone call from her mother." Starla gave herself a shake, struck by the heebie-jeebies. "Did you say choked?"

"It'll be fine. Remember, Janet wants me to do something for her, so we're good for a while." She thought back to the day Mrs. Godfrey had that pointless conversation at the theater, and wondered if she'd wanted to ask on Janet's behalf, but then thought better of it.

"Where is the statue now?"

"I locked it in the shop. I said a prayer as I left, but I don't know. I don't think," Rhee paused, her mouth dry. "I don't think our store was broken into yesterday."

"Why not?" Starla copied the page, handing the sheet of paper to Rhiannon while closing the book. "It wasn't Thor. It wasn't me."

"I think it was the statues, all three of them." Rhee nodded at her mother's surprised look.

"Are you – what?" Starla fanned her face with the book, color flushing her cheeks. "That's crazy. But not." She took a deep breath. "So what can we do?"

"I have to figure out who those spirits are."

"How?"

"I don't know just yet. Give me time."

Starla *humphed*, her bracelets still. "If my quilts get rearranged again, I will be one unhappy *bruja*."

"Understood."

Starla put her hand over her stomach. "Can those things leave the shop?"

Rhee shrugged again. "Maybe there's a reason J.W. sent them wrapped so tightly, and spelled. I thought he was concerned they might break. I could be totally wrong." She and her mom exchanged a look, for once reading one another's thoughts as clear as day. "I'll go get the packing tape."

"You are not going anywhere alone." Starla put her hand on Rhee's arm. "We'll wait for your Dad to get home."

A part of her sighed with relief. "Okay. Now, back downstairs and act like our only problem is Bonnie's confidence spell."

The two girls sat at the dining room table, and Rhee overheard them talking about Janet. And Jared.

They stopped quickly when Rhiannon crossed the threshold. Bonnie looked guilty, Mel studied her fingernails.

"What?" Rhiannon demanded. "You might as well spill it."

"I was just wondering what it would be like if Jared still had a thing for you," Bonnie admitted.

"Which he would, but you don't give him the time of day," Mel decided.

"Because I don't like him!" Rhiannon's cheeks flushed. "I don't."

Starla put her hand on Rhee's shoulder. "A girl's first kiss is impossible to forget."

"Mom, that is *not* helpful."

"It doesn't make what you feel for Dane any less. In fact, if you hadn't had those emotions for Jared, maybe you wouldn't have been ready for Dane." She shrugged. "Kismet."

"Jared is the past, and he needs to stay there," Rhee said in decisive tones.

"I know!" Bonnie put her hands together on the table, looking truly sorry. Rhee couldn't stay mad. "I was just saying, what if..."

"It might be nice for the Roberts to be miserable." Melody had no patience for the Roberts family, which hadn't helped her relationship with Jared's best friend, Caleb.

"Not from me. Remember,"

"I know. Karma." Melody blew out a breath.

"So, Rhee, I called Corey. He's going to come pick us up to go back to my house. My mom is making chicken and dumplings. You're invited but..."

"Thanks, Bon. I don't do the chicken, and I'm not sure about a dumpling."

"Mom said she can make you a salad."

"Thank you anyway. I appreciate you guys thinking of me, but I'll stay here and eat with Mom. Dad should be home soon." She handed over the spell. "Cleanse the rose quartz in salt water, don't forget. You are beautiful."

"Right." Bonnie's back straightened as if she headed into battle.

"Do you need anything, Mel?"

"I'm good, Rhiannon. I told you. Nobody is getting the jump on me."

Her mom looked startled, and Rhee knew she'd have to explain later.

"School tomorrow. English test too. Did you study, Rhiannon? Never mind," Bonnie laughed. "I don't know why I bother asking."

Rhiannon cleared her throat, uncomfortable. "I missed two questions last test. I'll be studying."

"You missed two?" Starla asked with suppressed mirth.

"Yes. My own fault, I admit. If you don't use certain sophomore English skills, like fragment sentences and freaking commas in the right places, it stands to reason I would be rusty. As I said, I'll be looking the study guide over carefully."

Melody laughed. "No offense, Rhee, but I am heartened for our school curriculum. I was almost sure you could ace it. Knowing you might miss a couple makes me love you that much more."

"Perfection is overrated," Starla agreed, barely controlling her laughter. "Right, honey?"

"Listen, perfection is not necessary, though I may strive for it. I find nothing wrong in reaching for the highest bar." Rhee crossed her arms over her waist, realizing she was the butt of their joke. Not mean laughter but sharing laughter.

She suddenly understood, quite clearly, the meaning of "I'm not laughing at you, but with you."

It still sucked.

"We're just teasing. And honestly," Melody said with a straight face, "I support your efforts. I know you work very hard."

"I know, I know," Bonnie added, giving Rhee a one sided hug. "But you're smart, you're beautiful, you have everything. If you get a B every once in a while, it just makes it more tolerable for the rest of us."

CHAPTER TEN

The front door opened, and Rhee dropped the book she'd been reading. "Dad!" She jumped up from the couch and gave him a giant hug.

"Wow, Rhiannon, I was only gone a few days. What's going on?" He laughed. "Not that I don't appreciate the greeting..."

"We've had some weird stuff happening, Dad." Rhee heard her voice, realizing she sounded a little too dramatic.

He pulled back, his dark eyes immediately turning serious. "What?"

"Everybody's okay. Come on, let's have this talk in the kitchen. Mom's baking. Apple pie, cookies. Singing to the oldies."

"Oh, no." Her dad followed her into the kitchen, which once again had become the heart of their home. "Starla?" He gave his wife a hug and resounding kiss, his hand at her waist.

"Miles! Welcome home, honey. Sit, sit."

"I was just telling Dad that we thought somebody broke into Celestial Beginnings."

"What?" Miles tilted Starla's face upward. "Rhiannon, you did not say anything like that. You said weird stuff."

"Stuff?" Starla sighed. "We have got to work on your vocabulary!"

"We're fine," Rhee said, in answer to her dad's confused expression. "We thought somebody broke into Celestial Beginnings."

"The shop was a total mess," Starla added.

"Did you call the police?" Miles kept his arm around his wife while studying his daughter.

"Yes. But Dad, we weren't broken into. I think there's a mischievous spirit, or maybe three, locked inside."

He backed up, his hip hitting the kitchen counter. "My accountant's brain would appreciate a clear, linear explanation of what you are talking about."

Rhee took a deep breath and told him everything from the beginning to when she and her mother refused to go out back without him. "I'm not sure what to do. It seems like they are playing tricks, I mean, Mom's merchandise was all over the floor but nothing actually broken."

"You were smart to lock the statues in." He frowned, his brows forming a V. "Can it get out? Are the animals all right?"

"We put Moonstone and Betsy back in the barn just a half hour ago. They didn't seem to notice anything wrong, but Dad, I can't pick up any paranormal energy. It's very strange."

"Can we send those things back?"

"I don't know. I think J.W. is closing his shop. You like antiques, Dad. Wait until you see them, if we can find them. Authentic. Certified. The whole bit. I'm hoping I can do a banishment spell and we can keep the statues."

Her dad scratched his chin. He kept a neat, black goatee that all her friends thought was cool. "Morpheus, huh?"

"We did some research. Morpheus has a Dream Wand and guides the dreamer through the Dream Gates. He decides what kind of sleep you'll have. If you pass through the ivory, the dream won't come to pass, but if you go through the horn, it will."

"Freud and Jung have nothing on this guy," Mom said with a laugh. "Edgar Cayce, either. I should have continued dream study."

"I am not a fan," Rhiannon declared. "I have enough going on without my sleep being interrupted on top of it."

"Cayce, Freud and Jung were all real men," her dad clarified. "Morpheus is a Greek myth."

"Head of the Oneiroi." Her mom sighed. "The cute one."

Her dad arched his brow. "What are Oneiroi?"

"Dream demons," Rhee answered, sensing her dad's frustration. "Nothing real."

"Rhiannon Selene, dream interpretation has been an ongoing study because what isn't 'real' during the day, or too frightening, or overwhelming, can be dealt with at night, in our subconscious. Freud swore that positive dreams enabled unsatisfied people to get through the hum drum of their waking hours without going crazy. Dreams are important."

"Really?" Miles grinned. "I thought Freud focused on unfulfilled fantasy."

Rhee rolled her eyes. "Dad, did you have to go there? We have rotten tempered spirits trapped in the shop! Who cares what some old pervert thought a hundred years ago?"

"Right, right." He nodded and buttoned his jacket, pulling out his gloves one at a time.

"He wasn't a pervert, Rhiannon. He was a noted psychologist. Brilliant man."

"Okay Mom. Can we just stay in the twenty-first century?"

"What do you want me to do?" Miles opened and shut drawers. "Why don't we have a baseball bat?"

"You wouldn't find it in with the silverware. Besides, I need you for moral support. You can't defend us from a non-physical being with a physical weapon."

"All right." He faced her and crossed his arms. "So what is the plan? From your tone, I'm assuming you have one."

"Sorry." Rhee fought hard against her tendency to be bossy. What did they expect from an only child? "First, we go to the shop and see if anything is messed up. If it isn't, we need to find all three of the statues and wrap them up, tight. We'll put a binding spell over them until I find out who the spirits are and how they got trapped."

"Someone else could have bound the spirits to the statues, which is why they are here?" Miles narrowed his eyes.

"Or a single spirit attached itself for some unknown reason. I don't think it's been bound. Otherwise, how could it create mischief?"

"A homing spell?" Starla snapped. "I don't know why I didn't think of that before. When we were kids, Grandma used a homing spell so we would never leave the yard."

"A witch's shock collar. What happened, Mom, did you get buzzed with electricity?" She waggled her fingers.

"Not me. I knew to stay in the yard." Starla shrugged. "The spell allows freedom of movement, but when it's time to rest, it brings the wanderer home."

"That makes sense." Rhee wondered if the same thing happened to the spirits. "I'm operating under the assumption that the way to keep the spirits confined to the statues is bubble wrap and tape."

"That I got," her dad said, walking into the laundry room and gathering supplies from the cabinet.

"I've got scissors!" Starla sang.

"Let's go." Rhiannon and her parents, on the same team. It felt really good.

They left the house out the back door and followed the path to the shop. It was a gray and cloudy Sunday afternoon, and spring seemed so far away. The weather added a layer of gloom that Rhee didn't really need.

Rhiannon reached the door, and because her parents were with her and they liked her to use her regular skills for things, she found the key in the hiding spot and slipped it in the lock.

With a twist, she inhaled and pushed the door open.

Her mom peered over her shoulder, while her dad looked over Starla's head.

"Do you see anything?" Starla whispered.

"Huh-uh. But I did say that blessing before I left." Rhee flicked on the light and walked inside, her parents on her heels. Literally.

Her dad scanned the room. He didn't have telepathic skills, like her mom sort of did. His magick was numerology, making him an excellent accountant. He also had fabulous fashion sense, which she inherited.

"It looks good," he said. "Am I missing something?"

"Everything in place," Starla agreed, walking toward the counter and the computer.

Rhiannon shut the door behind her, looking in the corners and up high on the shelves. "Where are they hiding?"

Miles, having followed Starla to the counter, found the framed document. "200 A.D., hmm? That would make these very valuable. And J.W. sent it wrapped in a regular box, in bubble wrap?" His brow lifted. "I would think crated with Styrofoam to protect them."

"There was a magickal protection spell." Rhiannon started searching the corners of the shop. "Here, Morpheus, Phobetor, and Phantasos," she called, the hairs on her nape standing at attention.

She turned abruptly, eyeing the shelves to the ceiling. It felt like they were watching her. Shivers traveled down her back, making her breaths come faster as adrenalin rushed. Fight or flight instincts bred for survival purposes warned her that she was in danger.

And should probably retreat.

"You called for me," she said aloud. "In J.W.'s dreams. Where are you now?"

"So you see them?" Starla asked.

Miles put his hand on Starla's shoulder, warning her to be quiet. His chin lifted, as if sensing danger himself.

Rhiannon bent down, looking under the couch, behind the cushions. "I can help you, if you want to go to the other side."

She sensed rather than heard a low chuckle. Glancing toward her parents, she realized they hadn't heard anything at all.

Closing her eyes, she thought, *I can help you.*

Her shields, carefully constructed against psychic invasion of her physical body and mind, twanged as a powerful force slammed toward her with such velocity that her entire body trembled.

"Rhiannon?"

She heard her mother's voice, from far away. Dr. Richards and Mrs. Edwards had taught her well. Self-protection, tighten the shield, be aware of the entity and its intent.

Her body stiff, alert, she bowed her head and closed her eyes. *You are not welcome in me. I can help you.*

I don't want your help, witch.

The voice tickled at her mind like soft tapping fingers across her forehead and over the top of her scalp. Envisioning a protective net of magical medieval chain mail, Rhee concentrated on closing her body as if she had a tube of super glue sealing each pore.

Which brother are you?

Its strength sapped at hers, stinging little bites, wearing her down as she held the spirit at bay.

I am the only one.

There are three brothers.

Rhiannon's body tensed as a ticklish sensation loosened her tight control. *Out!*

The entity laughed, pushing, tickling, wanting in her head.

Suddenly her mom's hand held hers, and her father held the others. They were three.

Out!

Witch.

With a pop, Rhiannon felt the release of power, suckled to her like tentacles. Drained of energy, she dropped to her knees, eyes going to the counter.

The three statues blinked blank oval eyes.

CHAPTER ELEVEN

"Wake up, honey," Starla cooed.

"You are safe," her dad said. "We've got the statue trapped."

Rhiannon sat up and rubbed her eyes, realizing she was on the couch in her living room and no longer in Celestial Beginnings. Had she dreamed of being in Greece? At a temple, with two winged men in togas?

"Just one? Where are the others?" Mentally doing a once over, she felt unencumbered of any psychical intrusion – then again, she'd thought the shop had been free of spirits in the first place. Maybe she needed to spend some time with Mrs. Edwards for a refresher course on how to talk to dead people.

Her dad scowled and pointed to the thickly taped cardboard box by the television. "One. Ugly guy with fangs."

Hadn't there been three statues on the counter? Rhee's memory fogged and her stomach felt queasy.

"You fainted. Out like a light, but your father caught you." Starla patted Rhee's knee, her fingers tapping in quick succession, as if her mother's energy needed a release. "You were so hot, burning up. I keep wondering what Einstein's mother must have thought as he grew up."

"Einstein?" Miles asked, bemused.

"You can't tell me that brilliant scientist had a *normal* childhood."

"I see." Miles put his hand on Starla's shoulder. "I thought we decided that normal was overrated?"

"I feel fine now," Rhee interjected, hearing the uncertainty in her own voice. Confusion sprang to the front of her emotions. What exactly had happened? She needed to write it down, record the feelings and compare them with her past experiences.

"We need to do a protection spell." Starla gestured to the candles and the goddess figurine set out on the family's altar. "As soon as you're ready."

"I forgot how quickly paranormal energy can act," her dad said, looking chagrined. "No matter how prepared I think I am."

"Thank you," Rhee said, blinking to clear her mind. "For adding your white light to mine." Something about the entity allowed it to be stronger than she'd been ready for. Her parents' quick thinking had helped protect her.

"Our lessons from the Institute came in handy. Think purity and strength." Her mom sighed, then folded her hands together to keep them still.

Rhiannon didn't remember fainting, or being carried back to the house. "The spirit said that he was the only one. When I argued, saying there were three brothers, it seemed to get angry. Called me witch." *Where were the other two statues?*

The phone rang, jarring them all into the present. "Let the machine get it," Starla stated, worry in her blue eyes. "I know that this is your passion, Rhee, but it seems dangerous. Why do you need to help this J.W.? Maybe you should let him deal with those nasty things."

"He is dealing with it, Mom. He sent them to me."

Janet Roberts' voice bellowed across the living room, her grating tones attacking Rhee's safe place on the couch.

"I'm calling to remind you about offering to help with the competition. Don't forget. The little kiddies are counting on you." With a cackle to put any bad witch to shame, Janet hung up.

Miles crossed his arms. "I was only gone a few days, not long enough for it to start snowing in Florida. Why are you helping Janet?"

Biting her lip, Rhee quickly explained. "It's your fault, really. Put out good, remember karma, yada yada. My first reaction was to tell her to jump in the lake."

Starla released a surprised laugh.

"Then I thought of you, Dad, and I agreed to help her make qualifications."

His eyes narrowed, though his mouth twitched with suppressed laughter. "I'll have to give the electric bull a tune up. And nobody's riding it without written permission from their parents." Miles rubbed his dark goatee, looking thoughtful. "I don't want a lawsuit, and I wouldn't put it past that family to make something up."

"I can't think about Janet right now." Rhee scratched the bridge of her nose. "Or what just happened in the shop. I still have to study."

Her dad dropped his hands to his sides. "Are you sure you're the same kid I had when I left?"

"Sarcasm does not memorize my study guide." Rhee got to her feet, giving the box a warning glance. "I think we should keep the statue in the box, tape it up, and lock the whole thing in the closet."

"I'm not ready to go back to the shop," her mom confessed. "But I'm not sure I want that thing in the house, either."

"It's fine," Rhee said, not really sure if she was telling the truth or not. "Remember how J.W. said the statues would end up back at The Magic Emporium after he sent them to the museum? They probably need to all three be together for true power, though. Keeping them separate should make them weak." Logically, anyway.

"How long in the closet?" Miles stared at the box as if it were filled with poisonous snakes.

"I'll call Tanya and then do the study guide, okay?" Rhee looked at her mother with hopeful eyes. "I'm starving. Potato soup? Cheese biscuits?"

Starla rubbed her hands together. "Nice comfort food. Give me forty five minutes and I'll give you a feast. Come on, Miles, you can help me chop and tell me about your trip."

Rhee watched her parents walk hand in hand to the kitchen with a warm heart. Ashe was a lucky soul. She looked forward to his arrival – but not to changing diapers, so much.

Walking up the stairs to her attic bedroom, she took out her cell phone and dialed Tanya. Her best Las Vegas friend and fellow psychic prodigy answered on the first ring.

"I had the weirdest feeling you were being attacked. I couldn't call," Tanya rushed her words, "because my mother has decided to take my phone on Sundays so she can have my full attention. And then she wonders why I prefer travelling the country to being in the same freaking house as her. Are you? Okay?"

Rhiannon laughed and opened the door to her room. "Yes. I have a rogue spirit I need to identify and get rid of. It tried taking me over, and it was so strong. Whatever this is has power – a lesser trained by fire psychic could have been hurt, I think." She shuddered.

"Explain."

Rhee did, then said, "So now Dad has it mummified and stuffed in a box. But its two brothers are still inside Celestial Beginnings."

"J.W. found you on the Institute's website?"

"Yeah." Rhee shrugged, though Tanya couldn't see it.

"And he couldn't find your home address, so he sent it to your mother's work address, which is public." Tanya spoke matter of factly, which Rhee appreciated. No drama queen antics, just truth.

"I think J.W. might be retiring, but I'm going to look him up. I meant to email Dr. Richards yesterday to ask if he'd heard of him and his Magic Emporium, but I just forgot."

"He's been busy, but I know he misses you. Don't forget!"

Rhee dropped on the edge of her bed. "I miss you all too. You want to know what's weird? When I woke up on the couch, after my faint, I dreamed I was in ancient Greece. Is that coincidence, with the statues being Greek? How am I going to find out who this spirit is while protecting myself?" She sighed. "I just don't know what it wants."

"Did you ask?"

"Yeah. No help. It said it wanted me."

"We can't blame Crystal Lake for this one, though it was on the tip of my tongue to do it anyway." Tanya giggled, the sixteen year old girl escaping for a minute. "I feel sorry for your parents sometimes. They just wanted you to have normal. Your destiny is so *not* normal."

"Maybe Ashe will be normal." Rhee highly doubted it.

"I highly doubt it," Tanya echoed. "So, any ideas on how to figure this out?"

Her friend's mental powers rivaled Rhee's. "We're going to try a binding spell, to keep the spirit attached to the statue so it won't be able to wander."

"That's a good start. I'll research the files at the institute tomorrow and talk to Dr. Richards. How are the shields holding?"

"Strong. I'm strong." Rhee felt it, down to her toes. "But honestly, I was surprised at the pressure the entity was able to exert. Mom and Dad jumped in to add good energy to mine. What if there are three brothers, three spirits, all working together?"

"Hmm. Three statues, three separate spooks. I guess bubble wrap them one at a time and see what happens." Tanya lowered her voice and asked in envious tones, "What are you doing tonight? Watching cool television shows? Laughing? Having fun? Eating food that tastes good?" She sighed. "I miss room service. We're traveling together this summer, right?"

"Yes! So long as Mom stays healthy, I will do one trip, not all the stuff Dr. Richards had posted. Gotta do the family thing." She actually liked doing the family stuff, and was only now coming to the place where she might admit it.

"I'd be more into it if I had *your* family."

Rhee murmured sympathetically. Tanya's germaphobe mother didn't understand her gifted daughter, and demanded they be together all the time. Unfortunately, her mother was also a terrible cook afraid of the germs in spices and bacteria in general.

"You are welcome here, any time."

"Do you need me to come hang out with you and the demons? Just say the word. I have plenty of frequent flyer miles."

"Morpheus is about a foot tall wearing a fig leaf and a bad weave, Phobetor has fangs and Phantasos looks sleepy. They all have adorable black wings, though."

Tanya burst out laughing. "Sounds like a party. Send pictures, Rhee. I'll get back to you in the morning."

"Two are missing in action, but I can send you a picture of the one we've got wrapped. Check out Wikipedia. Oh, I have an English test, so email me instead of text, okay? I always forget to turn off the sound and the teachers get mad." Tanya was the one person who would understand Rhee's embarrassment over getting any wrong answers, but Rhee decided to keep the goof up to herself.

"Got it. Say hello to Dane for me!"

Tanya hung up before Rhee could ask about Matthew, her other best Vegas friend and now Tanya's boyfriend. She wondered how things were going.

Being a teenager was hardcore stressful. Adding dating to the mix made everything more combustible. Rhee sent Dane a quick text saying she'd Skype him later with all the news, and then broke out the study guide. Ghosts, spirits or demons, she would get a hundred percent if she had to stare at the pages all night.

It was her own fault for not looking over the sheet last time, being so sure that she would know the information. Ego? Check it at the door. Rhee might be a world traveler, psychic prodigy and reality TV star, but at the end of the day, she was just like everybody else.

CHAPTER TWELVE

Rhiannon woke up before the alarm, her senses on high alert. Thor sat on the windowsill, his tail flicking back and forth. She immediately looked toward her closet, which had once been the home of an evil spirit holding other spirits captive.

A chill raced across her skin and she reached for her moonstone pendant. Since it tangled in her hair if she wore it while she slept, it hung across the vanity mirror.

She looked across the room and concentrated on the silver chain. With her palm outstretched, she telekinetically lifted the silver crescent moon and brought it to her by thought alone. The stone gleamed in the predawn light coming through the slats of the window, glowing with earth magick. Once it pooled in the hollow of her palm, she slipped the chain over her head. With a sigh of relief, she warded off any negativity.

"Thor? You see anything, big bad kitty?"

At his name, the cat thumped to the floor and padded heavily across the room, his fur puffed to let the world, both seen and unseen, know he was the bomb.

He meowed and leapt to her bed, purring.

Where had the dark energy come from? Had she dreamed again? Trying to remember gave her a headache, so after rubbing Thor's ears for a few minutes she got out of bed.

Her bare toes sunk into the furry white rug covering part of the white painted wooden floor. She loved her room, where she'd learned a lot about dealing with ghosts and spirits. Once a week she and her mother cleansed the space with sage, just to be certain that no bad energy remained.

"Might be time to do another cleansing," Rhee whispered with a shiver. "With some of the white cedar."

She dressed for self confidence, wanting to exude her own personal power against Janet's domineering force. Black jeans, black boots with a wedge heel, blue and black sweater with a cowl neck that showed off her moonstone pendant perfectly.

Brushing her wavy auburn hair, shoulder length after donating a good portion to locks of love a few months ago, she opted for a low ponytail over one shoulder and added silver crescent moon earrings. "We got a lot to do today, Rhiannon Godfrey," she told her image after swiping on a coat of light gloss. "Test, Tanya, Janet."

"Rhee, are you ready?" Her mom's voice trilled up the stairs like dancing mice in a Disney movie. "I made cheese toast."

Grabbing her backpack, she opened her bedroom door and ran down the stairs, accepting the napkin wrapped toast with a quick kiss to her mom's cheek. "You're the best."

"Good luck today. I wonder how Bonnie did with her confidence spell?"

Remembering her morning pep talk, Rhee had to laugh as she pointed to her pendant. "I'll have to tell Bonnie that I do one too. I just didn't realize it."

"Every morning," Starla chuckled. "As I'm slathering on moisturizer and praying to the Goddess that there isn't a new wrinkle. It's a woman's plight to doubt her beauty. You should use your science for that, Rhiannon."

"I have enough on my plate, thanks." She munched her toast and took her coat from the hook by the door.

"Too much loaded on that plate to study for your driver's test?" Miles swung the keys to his black BMW on one finger.

"Dad!" Rhee opened the door. "We're gonna be late."

They joked about her ambivalent attitude toward driving, which she really didn't have a good reason for. As usual, she promised to think about it, and as usual her dad caved in and said he really didn't mind taking her to school.

Once out of the car, she quickly found Bonnie and Melody where they waited for her by the front steps. They always walked together, if Corey didn't drive.

"Corey's got a stomach thing, which he swears is not the result of my mother's chicken and dumplings."

"They were awesome," Melody said, rubbing her belly.

"Someday you will realize you've been missing out." Bonnie spoke in sad tones. "On all of this wonderful meat."

"I don't think so." Rhee, completely on board with her parents' decision to avoid meat, had no problem with leather, but then again, she didn't have to chew it.

"Bonnie, how did you sleep?"

"Fine, but like I said, that dumb dream probably won't come around for another few months. I soaked the rose quartz in rock salt, though, like the spell said."

"Cool. If you need any help, just call."

Melody elbowed her. "Yeah, Bon, we know a local witch."

Rhiannon blushed. "I am not a witch." She immediately thought of Morpheus and the Oneiroi. One of the dream demons referred to her as a witch, too. "Not the pointy hat I'm looking to wear."

Practicing Wicca was something she slowly embraced, finding room in her life for psychic abilities and science as well as faith in the spiritual unknown.

She'd come a long way for a girl just turned sixteen.

"Are you ready for English?" Melody asked with a twinkle in her eye.

"I studied that guide until the font on the paper embedded itself on my brain."

Bonnie laughed and hugged her middle. "You'll do great, Rhiannon. I bet you don't miss another thing for the rest of the school year. I never saw anyone look so embarrassed over getting less than a hundred percent!"

"There is nothing to be embarrassed out, I promise. I do it all the time." Melody linked her arm through Rhiannon's. "So. Changing the subject to take the heat off of you, my friend, I got a letter from my dad."

"What?" Rhee and Bonnie asked at once, stopping to pull Melody to the corner beneath the stairs.

"Are you okay?" Bonnie put her hand on Mel's coated arm.

Melody shrugged. "Mom gave me the letter and made me read it last night once I got home from Bonnie's house, while she watched. She guarded the door like she was security or something."

Rhee imagined the scenario, knowing her friend had probably wanted to bolt rather than read her dad's letter. "Your mom's pretty smart."

Melody tossed her braid back over her shoulder. "He says he's getting out of jail at the end of the month, and he wants to see me."

"Are you going to?" Bonnie whispered.

"No."

Rhiannon's breath caught. "No?"

"Mom wants me to," Mel said angrily. "Wants me to give him another chance. Like she kept doing?" She shook her head, her eyes narrowed as she made a fist. "No thanks."

"And did your mom, well, support that?" Rhee didn't know what she would do in Melody's situation.

"No. But she said she understood, and warned me she's gonna be working on changing my mind. Which is why I told you guys about it, in case I need to sleep over a lot and stay out of Mom's way."

"Sure," Bonnie said as Rhee nodded.

"Ohh, whispers under the stairs," Janet sing-songed as she edged closer to them. "Does somebody have a crush on the football captain?"

"If we wanted you in the conversation, we would have invited you," Melody snapped, standing tall.

Janet actually took a step back.

Bonnie added, "We didn't invite you."

"Thanks for clarifying, Specs." Janet looked at Rhee. "Ready to talk?"

Rhiannon shook her head. "Not really. How long will this take?" She didn't want to give Janet any more time than necessary.

Janet thrust an envelope at her. "Take your unenthusiasm and times it by a million, and that's how I feel. If it weren't for..." She forced a smile. "Never mind. These are the girls on the team. First things first, you'll have to qualify on Saturday. Practice your bull," she paused, "and maybe say a prayer to whatever demon you acknowledge. Be at the fairgrounds by nine in the morning. You and I will have to carry the points for the other girls. Mostly me, but if you could help, that'd be a miracle."

Rhiannon blew out a breath, imagining cool, calming clouds covering her hot temper. Principal McGavin would not look kindly on Rhiannon if she got into a fist fight. Due to her absences, she was already on thin ice.

"You're going to have to be a little nicer than that. One more reference to my religion involving anything demonic, and I am done. Wiccans don't believe in the devil. But you make me really question that particular dogma."

Janet's eyes twitched but it was obvious she knew she'd crossed a line. "My bad."

"Is there anything else, or can we be done until Saturday?"

"Since we won't need the girls to practice until we know if we've made the team, we don't need to worry about them on the bull just yet. Saturday."

Janet left in a cloud of too sweet perfume.

"I really don't like her." Melody hitched her back pack up her shoulder.

"Me either." Bonnie glared in Janet's direction.

"I know I should try harder to understand her. I can't help but think the Goddess might cut me slack on this one."

"Let's go. We can finish talking at lunch," Mel said as the bell rang.

"Bye!" Bonnie went left, Mel went right. Rhiannon entered the crowd of kids moving down the hall in a tight knit herd, getting jostled from behind and bumping into...Jared.

He turned, startled. "Rhee? Are you all right?" He took her arm and pulled her from the herd.

"Yeah." She felt her face burn with embarrassment, downside of being a redhead. "My fault."

Jared's green eyes reminded Rhee of spring, not poison, like his twin sister. Kids avoided them like she and Jared were protected by an invisible force field.

"Thanks for helping Janet." He cleared his throat, obviously feeling the awkwardness between them. She could tell by the pink coloring his jaw.

She remembered his great sense of humor, and how he loved old Rocky movies, like her. When they'd dated, they'd laughed all the time. Until the smothering blanket of his family killed their sweet romance. "It's for the kids, like you told her I'd do. I hate to be so predictable." *I am confidant, I am capable.*

He laughed, his blond hair in loose waves that seemed wind-tossed to perfection. "It was a shot in the dark."

The air grew heavy. Jared studied her, and she was glad she'd taken the time to dress nice, and wear matching earrings. She looked at him, too, acknowledging his very, *very* cute factor.

First kiss. A thought sprang to mind as she looked at his mouth. *Another kiss?*

No. Rhee swallowed and stepped back, breaking the magic around them. She waved over her shoulder, hearing Jared's laughter follow behind as she practically ran toward her class.

CHAPTER THIRTEEN

"I aced the test, yeah for me, yeah for me," Rhee murmured, coming out of class. She'd known every answer. Studying worked.

Who knew?

She discreetly checked her emails, seeing one from Tanya, asking her to call. Dr. Richards had a story? Dang, she'd forgotten to email him again!

Rhee happened to like the older man's stories and decided to call instead, as soon as she got home. Rhiannon made her way outside the school. Her dad waited at the front of the line, so she didn't have time to talk to Bonnie and Melody. She hadn't told them about her and Jared's conversation when they'd gotten together for lunch. It felt, well, a teensy bit wrong. Besides, Mel's dad's unwanted intrusion in her life was more interesting.

"Hey." She slid into her dad's car, smelling the leather of the interior and the new vanilla incense.

"Hey yourself." He maneuvered through the parking lot, trying to avoid the mud splatter. It must have rained during the day because there were fresh brown puddles. "I spend more time at the car wash here than I ever did in Vegas."

"Do you miss it?" Rhee asked, pointing to the gray sky. "You gave up sunshine and paved roads."

"Not enough to go back. I don't feel like we are done here. Not like I *feel* like you do, but you know what I mean."

"Everyone has psychic ability. It's a fact."

"When I can win the lottery on a consistent basis, I'll believe you."

"Such a comedian!" Rhee checked the temperature gage inside the car that told the outside weather. "Sixty degrees. Practically a heat wave. How's Mom doing?"

"She spent all day online, tweaking the Celestial Beginnings website. She's very excited about expanding the business."

"Melody told me that internet orders are still up, and after the holidays, that's a big deal. Mel's pretty smart."

"I don't want your mom working too hard."

"Melody is ready to step in with more hours as soon as Mom gives the word."

Her dad nodded, pleased. "Starla is feeling so positive about this baby she even went paint shopping with me today. The guest room, Ashe's room, will be a warm blue."

"Blue is my color!" Rhee tapped the console between them. "And silver too," she said.

"It isn't your blue. Can you wait until you see it? We spent *hours* looking over paint samples."

Her dad sounded desperate so she relented a little. "You didn't buy the paint yet?"

"No."

"I'll reserve judgment." She sat back with a smile. So long as she kept her space upstairs, she really didn't mind what color they chose for Ashe's room.

They pulled to the front of the house. Her mom waited on the front porch, a giant ugly brown sweater around her shoulders. That particular sweater had come with her mother from childhood, and didn't get prettier with age.

Someday, Starla told Rhee, the sweater would be hers.

Rhee shuddered. "Why is Mom outside?"

"I don't know." Miles pulled to the front of the house. Rhiannon got out, dragging her back pack.

"How was the test?" Starla asked, hugging the sweater close.

"Fine. I got a hundred."

"Yeah!" She clapped her hands.

"Your lips are blue. Why are you out here?"

Her mom sighed. "It felt weird inside the house."

From the way her mom said weird, Rhee knew she was talking paranormal stuff. "Phobetor?" That wasn't good, if even boxed it emitted powerful vibrations.

Shrugging, Starla said, "I just didn't want to be in there. Alone."

Miles looked at Rhiannon. "We need to get this figured out today, or the statue gets to live in the lake." He took protecting his family very seriously.

"Dad, just wait. Tanya wants me to call her, she says Dr. Richards has a story that's somehow relevant to what's going on."

Her dad didn't look convinced, but turned to Starla. Her mom said, "Oh good. Dr. Richards will know."

Rhee shook her head. It hadn't been so long ago when Starla Godfrey and Dr. Richards butted heads like stubborn goats.

She bowed her head and said a prayer of thanks. It was a lot easier to get ahead in life when your mother and your mentor got along.

"Handle it, Rhiannon," her dad said. "This family is not taking any chances."

"I'm calling right now!" She whipped out her phone as they went through the door. Rhee got a shiver as she passed the closet where the statue was trapped in the box – taped and wrapped securely.

Or was that just wishful thinking on her part?

It occurred to her that the person she really needed to talk to was J.W. himself. Why hadn't she thought of that before?

Tanya answered right away and Rhee shook one arm, then the other out of her coat before taking a seat on the couch.

"Well?" Having a psychic BFF cut down on regular conversation. Short hand worked in a pinch.

"Dr. Richards is very familiar with Morpheus, and all the legends. He thought it strange that this particular entity was coming to you while you were awake, since Morpheus is a dream messenger."

Rhee sank into the cushions, putting her phone on speaker so her parents could hear too. "I thought so – nothing physical, more intuitive."

"Gotta learn to trust your gut, Rhee."

"Tanya, I like proof. It's part of who I am."

"Like I don't know that?" Tanya laughed. "Dr. Richards suggested you capture the entity, which it seems like you've done, and-"

The closet door blew open with a resounding crash.

"What was that?" Tanya asked.

Rhiannon stared at the open door and the box that catapulted from the interior.

Starla sat next to Rhee while Miles stood over them with his chest out. "The statue," Rhee said, her heart hammering behind her ribcage.

"I don't understand."

Tanya's calm, cool voice prodded Rhiannon into observation mode. "The box the statue was wrapped in, and kept in the closet while we decided what to do, is now in the foyer. While we were talking the closet door seemed pushed open from the inside. The box is still sealed."

"Nobody is in the closet?"

Rhiannon started to say no, but then looked at her dad. "Is there someone in there?"

He picked up the lamp and walked toward the box, and the open closet. Peering in, while keeping clear of the box, he shook his head.

"No. Nobody inside."

"Good. Now, what is happening with the box?"

"It's still."

Tanya exhaled. "You're going to have to open it."

Rhiannon's toes curled inside her cute wedge boots. Her moonstone pendant lit up like a Christmas light. "That is the last thing I want to do."

"I get it. I'll stay on the phone with you. Have your dad video with his phone, so we can talk. I don't want to risk losing the connection."

Mouth dry, chest tight, Rhiannon nodded at her dad.

"Let's get the box outside. Out of harm's way."

"Dad, we have to keep this statue bound, not let it escape."

Chin taut, he opened his phone, and hit the record button. "I don't like this." He looked into the screen. "For the record."

"Got it. Dad, capturing this on film is the best way to keep us safe." She looked at her mom. "You gotta let go of my arm."

Starla did, reluctantly.

Rhee got up. Walked to the box. "Dad, you taped this as if it carried the plague inside it."

"It might," Tanya confirmed. "Be careful."

"Wait." Starla stood, her shoulders straight, her voice firm. "Maybe we should open it within the sacred circle? Protect ourselves with white magick."

Impatient, Rhiannon shook her head and ripped a layer of tape off the top. All of a sudden the television blared on and the lights flickered. The stereo in the kitchen blasted Oldies music and the phone rang as if...possessed.

Rhiannon, her mom and dad all looked at one another in surprise. Rhee gathered her considerable psychic power and shouted, "Stop!"

It was as if she'd flicked a switch.

The house went dark. Quiet.

Her quick, hard breaths sounded especially loud as she calmed herself from the surge of adrenalin. She looked at her parents. "Are you all right?"

They each nodded, her mom at her dad's side, her dad holding his phone in one hand, and the lamp in the other, as if it were a weapon. How many times did she have to remind him that he couldn't fight the nonphysical with the physical?

"Me too." Except for feeling like she could run a five minute mile, which is what happened after having all that energy at her fingertips. She looked at her phone. "We lost Tanya. My phone's dead."

"Mine too," her dad said, tossing it to the couch and putting his free hand on Starla's shoulder.

"I should probably call her back. I have an extra battery upstairs." She looked toward the stairs, reluctant to walk up them alone. But at sixteen she was way too old to ask her parents to come with her. "I can't believe that happened." She wasn't sure exactly what *had* happened.

Starla, looking very pale in the dim light, pointed to the box. "It's open, Rhiannon. Did you do that?"

"Huh uh." Rhiannon's stomach clenched as she walked over to the box and carefully pulled back the flaps.

"Well?"

"Phobetor is gone."

CHAPTER FOURTEEN

The three of them went to the back of the house and flipped the breaker, nobody worrying about being called a chicken, since they were all feeling the same.

Once the lights were on, they did a thorough search of the house, looking in every nook and cranny for the Phobetor statue.

Starla took a broom stick and poked under the couches and in the corners, while her dad checked the shelves, her attic bedroom, and the basement. "It can't be in here," her mom said with a frustrated jangle of her stacked bracelets.

"It couldn't have gotten outside!" Miles brushed a dust fuzzy from his shoulder. "Everything was locked tight."

"We're dealing with the paranormal, guys, remember? There are no rules."

Leaving her parents plotting vengeance in the kitchen, she went upstairs to her room and called Tanya back, explaining what happened.

"You are dealing with a very intelligent entity," Tanya said. "It knew enough to distract you rather than risk pitting its energy against your family's combined white magick."

"I think it just wanted out. Dad said he hadn't wrapped the statue because he'd wrapped the box. Now we know. The figurine has to be completely mummified."

"If you can find it!"

"You sound like my mom." She shivered. "Listen, what story did Dr. Richards have to share? I have to figure this out or my mom won't sleep, which means my dad will be furious."

"You still don't sense danger?"

"No! I must be off base, but I'm not seeing it. Maybe Dr. Richards' story will help."

"He says to read up about the Dream Messenger – he's wondering if you should go to sleep, and open your mind to dreaming. Maybe the entity will be able to communicate that way. You know, keep a pen and paper by your bed and jot down every last detail of what you remember when you wake up."

"I like my dreams to be filled with milkshakes and bad 60's album covers, not dark little dream demons using my brain as a call center." She flipped through the pages of her dog-eared fashion magazine, not really looking at the clothes.

"It was just a suggestion, Rhee." She paused. "Though you don't really have a lot of other options if you can't find the statues." There was another pause. "Are you reading Teen Vogue? I loved the boots on page 78."

Rhee laughed and tossed the magazine on the bed. "Creeper. I'm going to have to go back to the shop. I don't have time for dreaming. I'll try going by myself this time, and see what happens if I'm alone."

"Bad idea, oh brilliant one," Tanya said without a trace of teasing. "You needed your mom and dad's energy against the spirit. What if it is three, like you thought?"

"I know now to be better prepared. I have my moonstone, and I'll do a full body protection spell before I go inside. I just think I might have a better chance at finding them, if I don't have anybody else with me."

"Not good reasoning, Rhee. And if someone else was telling you this, you would be on my side of the argument."

"I'm fine!" Rhee bristled, a little annoyed that her best friend didn't appreciate her spook skills. "I've gotten very strong. You'll see."

"This isn't a competition."

Rhee smacked her forehead, forgetting about her ego and remembering her promise. "Thanks for reminding me. I've got to go practice on the bucking machine."

"What? I thought you hated that thing? It knocked your spine out of alignment and you walked with a limp for two weeks."

"Do you have to remind me?" Hard to do heels when your left foot drags. "I'm doing a favor for Janet," she explained.

Tanya's silence shouted around Rhiannon like red chaos.

"Tanya?" Rhee questioned, wondering if the line had gone dead again.

"I'm here. Stunned. Did you say you were doing a favor for Janet? Your super arch enemy?"

Rhiannon laughed self-consciously. "Yes. Not just for her, but the integrity of Crystal Lake High with the added benefit of sending kids to this really awesome camp."

"You are such a sucker."

"That's what I said!" At least she'd gotten Tanya away from the subject of Rhee going to the shop alone. Which she knew she had to do, if she was to find those statues and capture them.

"Well," Tanya asked, "Do you still have all those pads and the helmet and everything?"

"Yeah, unfortunately I do. Dad said he'd tune the machine for me, so I guess I better go remind him. I have to be ready by Saturday to stay on for at least ten seconds. I think. I'll need to read the rules again. I was much more motivated when I did it to prove I could!"

"A grudge match. You should show Janet up, and win this time." Her sigh resonated with happy memories. "That was so awesome, last year at the fair. Cotton candy. Don't you remember I bobbed for apples? I never did tell my mom about that."

"Which is why we are both still alive today." Rhiannon stared outside her window overlooking the front driveway. Her skylight allowed filtered gray into her room. Living in Washington State sure made her appreciate the occasional sunny day. "Is it warm?"

"A perfect seventy five degrees," Tanya said. "I don't envy you your weather. So, do you think Janet might want to be your new best friend?"

"I have a best friend. You – like it or not." Rhee smiled, and sat down on the chair next to the window. "You have no idea how pained she looked, having to ask me for a favor. Then Phobetor tried choking her. I think I agreed just to get her out of the shop."

Rhee had to find those pesky statues before her dad really did make her throw them in the lake. Crystal Lake was the recipient of all sorts of things – one time she'd even seen the rusted skeleton of a car.

"Some humble pie will do her good. We are best friends, and I like it a lot. And I know you aren't going to listen to my advice."

Busted.

"So, promise me you will at least text me once you go over there, and then when you get back. I want to know you're safe. 'Kay?"

"Fair enough." Her phone made a bleeping noise and she looked to see who was calling. "Oh, hey, this is Dane. I want to take this. We've barely talked in days."

"Sure, sure. Tell him I said hi. And text me!"

Tanya hung up, and Rhee answered Dane's call. "Dane, how are you?" Her heart skipped in anticipation of a good conversation.

"Excellent, now that I've finally gotten a chance to talk to you. All text, no talk. How are things going in Rhiannon World?"

His voice warmed her from the toes up. "I am not an amusement park."

"Can you imagine the line if you sold tickets to your world? A little magic here, a ghost over there. We could make millions."

She knew he was joking, and hesitated over telling him the entire truth. "Promise not to get too mad?"

"Okayyyy."

She hesitated, then blurted out her plans for Saturday morning. "I promised Janet that I'd ride broncos with her. It will just take a few hours and I'm so sorry to take time away from being with you,"

He interrupted her heartfelt apology with a burst of laughter. "This I have got to see. I mean, the pictures your folks have of you on that bronco is one thing, but to see you all gussied up in cowboy boots and a hat? Hanging on for the ride of a lifetime as some horse tries to buck you off?" He laughed harder. "I am so not mad."

Rhee stiffened. "To think I was worried you might be bored. I didn't realize you would find it quite so funny."

"I'll bring the video camera."

"You will not!" Her cheeks burned. "This is just to qualify. It's not like I'm any good."

"Don't ruin this for me, Rhee. I have the best image in my head right now. Can you do me a favor and twirl your hat in the air as you hang on with one hand?"

The image was so cartoonish that she couldn't help but laugh too. "No. Not unless you want me to break my neck."

"Absolutely not. Hang on with both hands." He quieted, then went back to chuckling. "I can't wait to tell Dad."

"I like your dad. Glad to be a source of amusement." She cleared her throat. "So, if you're through mocking my bronco abilities, do you remember how I told you about those Oneiroi statues I got from a guy who follows my work at the institute?"

"Yeah?"

"I think they're possessed."

124

"What?" Dane released an exaggerated exhale. "Only you, Rhiannon."

"I know." She shrugged, then stood and paced her room. "It makes sense he would send them to me, knowing I deal with ghosts and spirits, I suppose."

"I'm not so sure. It seems random. Why pick you out of all the other psychics in the world? No offense, Rhee, but you don't even drive yet."

"What does that have to do with anything?" As if driving a car made her a better psychic? She stayed on the conversational tangent. "The Oneiroi, not just the three main brothers, but I guess there's thousands, like a bunch of bats emerging from a cave night to guide people's dreams, are dream demons. Anyway, J.W. asked to be guided in a dream for where to send the statues, and they picked me."

"You got the popular vote from some demi gods?"

"Well, Morpheus is the one who comes to deliver messages in dreams. According to myth. I haven't seen him."

He sighed deeply, sadly. She absorbed his sorrow and knew he remembered his dead twin, Dennis.

"Dennis used to communicate with me in my dreams. He couldn't talk, unless I was sleeping and then it was like nothing was wrong. We talked about everything." His voice lowered. "I miss him."

"I know." They shared a binding moment of silence before Rhee asked, "Do you regret that his spirit crossed over to the light?"

"No. No, Rhiannon, he deserves peace. I will never forget how you helped with that."

"If you were here, I'd give you a big hug." Rhiannon spoke softly, imagining she could wrap her arms around his waist and hold him close.

"Thanks, Rhee." He cleared his throat. "I didn't mean to be such a downer."

"Not even close, Dane. It's okay to feel sad. And hopefully there's comfort in knowing his soul is at rest." It seemed a consistent thread in her work that a freed spirit, once it moved to the other side of whatever energy held it captive, rested peacefully.

"I imagine his smile, his laugh. He had a quirky sense of humor."

"Like you? Part of Dennis lives in you, just by the memories you have of him."

"That is a very cool thought. Thanks."

She moved the subject away from the tender past. "I'm only sixteen, without a driver's license - as you continue to point out - but I've spent my entire life working with the paranormal. I accept the idea of the statues being inhabited by spiritual energy. Is it a ghost who kicked the mortal bucket and decided to hang out?" She walked her room, end to end and back, the phone tucked between shoulder and ear. "Not a ghost. There was coherent thought and action. Spirit, then – but malevolent, or relatively friendly?"

"There's no such thing as Casper, Rhiannon. You have to be careful."

"I know." She thought of going to the shop, alone, and a chill traipsed down her spine.

"What are you planning?" Dane broke in.

Rhiannon had forgotten for a moment that Dane could pick up her thoughts. His psychic capabilities only worked around other psychics. "Uh, nothing."

She knew he wouldn't want her going into the shop by herself either. Nobody seemed to trust in her abilities to take care of herself, and it was starting to get annoying.

"Rhee." His tone let her know he didn't believe her.

She had to tell the truth. "I want to run over to the shop, that's all."

"Why?"

Straightening her shoulders, she forced herself to stop acting like a wuss. "Because I think I will have a better chance getting the spirit to contact me if I am by myself. No distractions."

He paused. "Are you wearing your moonstone?"

She relaxed a little. "Yes."

"I want you to call me as soon as you get done, okay? It isn't that I don't think you can do it, I just worry that something outside of your control might happen. It's never a bad idea to have a spotter."

She laughed, imagining lifting weights with a spirit. She wouldn't trust its grip. "I wouldn't let any of the entities I've met hold my weights."

"I was talking about me, your in the flesh boyfriend."

She stopped walking. "You are in Montana."

"I don't suppose this can wait until Friday?"

"I don't think the spirits will let me wait that long." She took a step toward the window, looking outside. "And I know my dad won't."

CHAPTER FIFTEEN

Rhee got off the phone with Dane, and went downstairs. Her parents were in the living room, watching television before dinner. She tiptoed quietly passed them and down the hall by the laundry room, grabbing a coat from the hooks on her way outside.

Imagining a protective white shield around her entire body, she walked the path to Celestial Beginnings. No lights were on, making it look like a giant spooky barn instead of the cozy New Age store her mom had created.

Dusk, that half hour or so between afternoon and night held mystical properties, as if a veil was lifted in time. No moon, no sun, just gray shadow.

Maybe brushing down Moonstone and Betsy would be a better idea than going inside...No, she chided herself. She was a medium coming into her own. How else would she get stronger if she didn't practice?

She faced the door, adrenalin racing through her like chocolate covered espresso beans.

I can do this.

Opening the door with her mind, she waited at the threshold, turning on the lights, one by one, banishing shadowy corners.

She stepped inside.

Hello?

Silence lay heavy in the air.

The sound of her boots on the wooden floor echoed as she walked toward the counter. The basket of stuffed kittens by the register, the framed certificate of authenticity for the marble figures, the cup of pens were all exactly where she'd left them.

So where were the Oneiroi?

Hyper aware of the silence, of the millions of shadowed niches within the old barn, Rhiannon walked slowly across the floor.

Where are you?

Instinctively, she realized she wasn't alone, but the mysterious entities weren't talking.

You wanted me. Can I help you with something?

She heard a sound back by the counter and whirled, her hair standing up on her arms. "Hello?"

Another sound from her left made her turn in the opposite direction. And another from a third position.

Surrounded, she thought. Well, I am surrounded too. By white magick. She remembered a time when she might have run in fear, but that time had passed. She knew to stand her ground. Centered. Solid.

Was that a black wing hiding in the quilts?

She walked toward the pile of blankets, determined to catch one of the statues, if not all of them. She flicked the fabric back, hand poised. Nothing was there.

Faint laughter danced in the air. "So you think this is funny? Great, I'm used to scary spirits, not ones with a sense of humor."

The basket of kittens fell to the floor with a violent shove, knocking even the idea of a joke out the door.

Her toes curled in her boots as she crossed her arms over her stomach. "Come on out. I'm ready."

The kittens began to lift, first one, then another and finally a third. Just like Corey had done earlier, the kittens juggled in the air.

Rhee's scalp prickled. The entities had been watching, studying their behavior. "Nice trick," she said. "Almost as good as Corey."

The kittens went faster, higher. Rhiannon couldn't pick up any psychical energy, even as she watched quite clearly the stuffed animals tossed by invisible hands.

Was the entity taking the shape of a human? The thought made her rethink her position on confronting them alone. "Who are you? Morpheus?"

She edged toward the door. The kittens, still being rotated in a circular motion, followed her movements, letting her know the entity was also keeping a close eye on her. Talented, and she wasn't talking about the juggling.

Swallowing hard, Rhee reinforced her psychic shields and tossed in a prayer to the Goddess while she was at it. "What do you want? To show me how strong you are? To wow me with your juggling skills? I am not impressed."

She crossed her arms and did her best to look bored.

The stuffed kittens fell to the floor in a heap, and Rhiannon was finally able to feel a blast of psychic energy as the spirit flew toward her in a gust of hot air.

It smelled musty, old, like the stink when she and Melody had first opened the box from J.W.. Trained to identify and catalogue scents, temperatures, anything that might give a clue to the identity of the spirit, Rhee forced herself to remain still and aware as invisible fingers lifted the ends of her hair.

Cold foreign energy tickled across her cheek, as if someone had brushed their knuckles across her flesh. She couldn't help the goose bumps that broke out along her skin.

She heard more laughter. Diabolical, and Rhee knew she was being tested. That made her angry.

"You came to me. Stop playing games, and tell me what you want."

The air rushed around her, so powerful it blew her clothes back and twisted her hair.

She braced her feet, her body. "Is this all you got?"

The teasing feel of the energy stopped, becoming darker. Bolder. The kitten's glassy button eyes gleamed from the floor where they lay, and Rhee backed up as she realized they were getting to their little stuffed feet. Tails lifting, the dozen or so toys lined up, and stared her down.

The fear that she'd sworn she wouldn't feel blossomed like a wet sponge and her mouth dried.

These toys wanted to hurt her, she knew it. It didn't make sense, but then again, it didn't have to. Malevolence seeped like a mist. Slowly, they moved toward her, a dark line of demonic lavender energy. They walked with foul intent and Rhee inched closer to the door.

Her only thought now was retreat.

She glanced away from the kittens, who moved quicker, separating themselves into smaller groups as they tried to cut off her escape.

She held up her hand, telling them to stop.

They didn't listen to her tone of command, probably because her voice trembled. One of the kittens leaped up and bit her, drawing blood on her palm.

"Ouch!" Since when did stuffed animals have teeth? She remembered Phobetor's fangs.

The rest of the kittens, perhaps scenting her blood, or that she was really afraid, all jumped at her with claws they shouldn't have and tiny sharp teeth.

She shook them off, kicking one across the room as she ran now for the door. She'd let her magic slip, and the little demonic kittens had gotten to her. Bites, nips, cuts, she pulled on the door as dark energy pushed against it, not allowing her to leave. She twisted the knob, stepping on the purple cats wings and pulled the door open.

Free.

The kittens couldn't cross the threshold, but she could. Rhee ran back to the house with jumbled emotions and bruised pride. A dozen tiny cuts stung.

This changed things, this, this was dangerous. She faced her parents as they sat in front of the television, showing them her hands. "We need to stay away from the shop for a while, okay? I have to figure this out."

"What is going on? Did you go there alone?" Her dad stood, hurt, and angry. "I forbid you to pull that stunt again, Rhiannon. We had a deal, that we work as a family."

Her mom looked disappointed, which was worse than her dad's words.

CHAPTER SIXTEEN

They went to the kitchen, where her mom took out the first aid kit above the refrigerator. Blue eyes not so sparkly, her mom looked at her and shook her head. "What were you thinking, going in there by yourself? Sit."

Starla dabbed at the cuts with tea tree oil, a natural antiseptic that made Rhee smell like eucalyptus. "This family has been through enough this winter to make the angels cry. We've all cried." Her mom patted a cut on Rhee's hand, wincing when Rhiannon sucked in a breath. "If you get hurt, how do you think your father and I feel?"

"I wanted to help!" They couldn't have the statues show up inside the house, what if her mom was hurt, or her dad, or worse, Ashe?

"By sacrificing yourself?" Her dad scowled. "Very over the top, even for you."

Her father's critique held a harsher sting than the tea tree oil. "I wanted to make myself available, for communication. J.W. said the Oneiroi chose me." She bowed her head, determined not to cry. She'd known going into the shop would be something her parents wouldn't allow, so she'd snuck by them. Now she had to pay the price of their concern. The older she got, the more she understood that there were other people to consider besides herself. Blah.

"I don't like it," Starla announced, packing up the kit and handing it to Miles to put away.

"When I was inside the shop, I felt tested, as if this has a personal connection." She looked at the tiny cuts on her hands and remembered the malevolent energy focused on her. "Like facing me might be some sort of challenge for them."

Miles pointed angrily at her cuts. "First round goes to them. No more playing lone wolf. Do we need to send you to Las Vegas?"

"Dad!" Sending her away? "I need to capture those statues."

"I mean it. You've been trained, but my understanding is that no two spirits are going to be the same. There will be some, like this one, who are stronger than you. Period. It happens. Accept it. Deal with it. You've let your pride interfere with common sense."

Rhee bit the inside of her cheek, knowing her dad was right, but not liking it so much. The clock on the wall rattled.

"So," Starla put her hand on Rhee's head, smoothing the tangles. "Let's make a plan. I don't need anything in the shop until Saturday. We can decide how to handle the hostile take-over after dinner."

"So long as they stay there," Miles said with a threatening frown. "Do you think that's where our little demon went? Back to his brothers?"

It was hard not to hold a grudge and stay mad, but Rhiannon gave a short nod. "I think so." She shrugged and confessed, "Actually, I don't know. It makes sense to me that the three need to be together, but I've only heard one voice."

Starla stirred the soup, bringing the rich scent of potato, cream and a hint of crushed red pepper alive.

Suddenly starving, Rhee looked across the kitchen to her stiff dad. He rarely showed his temper, but she'd managed to make him pretty mad, too.

"Sorry, Dad."

His black eyes flashed, and she saw the love for her in them before he blinked and relaxed. "Me too. We're a team. Godfreys. Got it?"

"Okay." She blew out a breath. "So, team Godfrey has to practice the mechanical bull. I promised Janet I'd do well enough to qualify, which is ten seconds. Minimum. I can go out after dinner, if you remembered to tune it up?"

"Sure did," her dad said with a satisfied smile. "Used that new wrench you bought me for my birthday."

Starla cleared her throat and her parents exchanged a parental look. "We will go with you," her mom said.

Rhiannon accepted that her wings were clipped, for at least a little while. Thanks a lot, J.W.. "Hey, how about I call that guy? Ask him what's going on?"

"That is a brilliant idea," Starla said, getting bowls from the cupboard and putting them on the table.

Her dad handed her the iPad she'd forgotten to put away. "See if he's listed."

Rhiannon typed in J.W's Magic Emporium in Kansas City. The website popped up first on the search engine.

"He's for real." She started to feel a little better, closer to getting answers.

Her dad looked over her shoulder and started to laugh. "I think I like him. Mummified bodies, enchanted books, a three headed pig. I bet his store is something else."

Starla looked over Rhee's other shoulder. "I would love to see his place. It must be stuffed with curiosities."

"Road trip?" Rhee suggested, wondering how else they'd manage to cross the country with the statues.

"No trips. Just call." Miles nodded. "Where's the number?"

Rhiannon had already gone to the website, searching for a contact number. Starla handed Rhee the receiver for the kitchen phone, and didn't seem to mind too much when Rhiannon telepathically dialed.

"It's ringing. Man, I have so many questions."

The phone rang and rang.

And rang.

"No answering machine."

Disappointed, Rhiannon hung up. "He did say he was closing his shop."

"He should still check for messages." Starla shook the ladle, clearly upset.

"We can try again after dinner," Miles offered. "And keep trying, until somebody answers."

After dinner, the results were the same. Rhee went to call Dane and Tanya to let them know how the experiment went, and realized she couldn't find her phone.

"Oh no." Had she dropped it in the shop? Was it worth running inside to get?

"Yeah. Gotta have my phone." Scratching her nose, she went to tell her mom, and overheard her parents arguing.

"I don't want her facing this kind of thing, and I don't want you involved either," her dad said. "We have to protect the baby."

Guilt nibbled at Rhee's conscious. Had she endangered her family by seeing spirits? So far they were learning, together. Rhiannon hadn't asked to see ghosts, or have paranormal powers. She'd tried not to use them, but that hadn't worked out.

"Celestial Beginnings is a business, Miles," her mom answered sharply. "I can't do much from inside the house. Rhiannon and I can do a sage and rosemary cleansing of the shop, we've done them for her room, and that spirit who'd trapped Suzanne was mean."

"I can do it," her dad said.

"You can certainly help, but it is a Goddess blessed duty, and is more powerful coming from a woman. Which you are not."

"Thank you."

Before her parents started off on another tangent, Rhee interrupted by tapping at the door frame. "Uh, I forgot my phone."

"Where?" Her dad asked suspiciously.

"I think I dropped it in the shop."

Starla put her hands to her cheeks. "Oh."

"Can you mentally bring it to you?" Her dad didn't like her using her gifts, but he was more practical about it.

Rhee nodded. "Yes, if I'm standing outside our house, I think I can go that far. But that means opening the door to the shop. We should probably be prepared for flying stuffed kittens."

"And asking you to leave your phone would be like asking you to cut off your arm?" Miles stared at her with his dark eyes.

Swallowing hard, Rhee said, "That's about right. I have friends, and homework, and Dane and,"

Her dad sliced his hand in a stop motion. "Starla, stay here. I'll go stand with Rhee."

Her mom rose, her face set. "Miles, I appreciate you wanting to protect us, but this baby will be born into a magickal family, which means that if he is to survive with us, he will be exposed to these things. Not that I would go in direct danger, but there is no sense hiding from every shadow."

Rhee couldn't believe her scared of every shadow mom just said that. Her dad's chin jutted out, but then he gave a slow nod. "If you're sure?"

Starla exhaled. "Very. Thank you, honey."

"I can do this, you guys," Rhiannon said, feeling guilty.

Neither of her parents answered her as they walked out the back door. The outdoor lights over the barn gave some reprieve to the black country night. The moon began its ascent to the sky and the stars glittered like diamonds.

"Hurry," Starla said, rubbing her arm against the chill. "I'm freaking myself out."

Miles put a comforting hand on her shoulder. Rhee concentrated on mentally unlocking the shop door. Twisting the handle. Slowly, slowly opening it while calling silently for her phone. Open about five inches wide, the door trembled with Rhee's power. She held her breath, not wanting to alert the energies inside the shop that she, at least psychically, was inside. Her phone quivered out the small width between door and frame, and floated toward her. She couldn't make it move any faster. Inch by inch, it had come half way toward her when they heard cackling sounds coming from within the cavernous shadow of the shop.

Three statues, piled one on top of the other, peered out of the dark with shiny blank eyes and pointed black wings.

"Look." Rhiannon gulped. "Do you see that?" Goosebumps raced over her body, too scared to land in one spot.

"I think we found the statues," Miles said in a grim voice. "All three, like you thought, Rhee."

Starla, with surprising strength, straightened her shoulders and raised her hand toward the shop. "They cannot have Celestial Beginnings. I made that business myself."

The dream demons laughed.

"They think they can." Rhee stared at them, searching for some clue as to what they might want.

As soon as the phone was close enough, Rhee grabbed it and mentally slammed the door closed, with all her strength.

"Did you get them?" Her mom's voice held no quarter.

"I wish, but they're crafty little devils." Rhee pressed her phone to her chest. "They probably jumped back in time."

The Godfrey family went back inside the sanctuary of their home. "We are safe in here." Starla's words offered no room for argument.

Rhee couldn't explain it, but she agreed, anyway. "I think so too. Maybe the three need to be together to have any sort of real power."

Miles shrugged. "I'll still double check all the doors and windows, just in case."

"I'm calling Dr. Richards." Rhiannon didn't give herself time to second guess, scrolling through her contacts until she found his name. She pushed call, and he answered on the second ring.

"Rhiannon! Tanya said you I might hear from you. How are the Oneiroi?"

"Nasty little beasts, Doc. They've gotten free, and have control of Mom's shop." It felt good talking to someone who had more experience in these matters than she did.

"Oh. Well, J.W. didn't say anything about them being possessed." He exhaled. "I should have figured, though. He has a thing for spirits."

"You know J.W.?" It would have been nice if the man had said so in his letter.

"Sure, he's had me debunk a few of his curiosities. Some of them were real, too. He's a true collector, you know. Does it for the love of the treasure hunt."

"We gathered from his website and cryptic letter," Rhee said. "But I tried calling his number. He doesn't answer."

"He was talking of retirement when we spoke last year."

Everything matched what she knew. "Did he tell you he would send these statues to me? And why? And what the heck am I supposed to do with them? They're too vicious to be pets."

Rhiannon brought him up to speed on everything that had happened so far. After reminding her that ego was man's downfall, and pride caused more harm than good, Dr. Richard's suggested a binding spell.

"That's what we were thinking too, but now I can't catch them. They're loose."

"My suggestion is to avoid the shop for the next day or so, and I will see what I can find. Have you been dreaming any strange dreams since receiving them?"

"Not really. After I fainted I thought I had dreamed of Greece."

"They are Greek gods, so that makes sense. Anything particular?"

"No. Not unless they are in cahoots with Nancy Sinatra."

CHAPTER SEVENTEEN

Rhiannon surprised herself by how easy it was to forget about the dream demons locked in the shop. Out of sight, out of mind.

Instead, she focused on school, stretching her sore muscles from her hour of practice on the bull, and dreading the upcoming weekend.

Practice reminded her that she didn't like whipping around out of control, squeezing all of your muscles tight as you attempted to stay relaxed so you didn't actually hurt yourself. Bronco riding was seriously complicated.

It didn't help that she seemed to see Janet, or worse, Jared, each time she went down the hall from one class to the other. Lunch? Jared. Remember awkward attraction. English? Janet. Remember deep seated dislike.

She wished she'd stayed home.

"Come over to my house after school," Melody offered. "I always go to your house. Mom actually baked cookies, so we have snacks. I'm telling you, something is very weird with her."

"I'm coming too," Bonnie said. "This will be fun!"

Rhiannon knew if she went home, she'd have to deal with the demon spawn in the shop, or practice the bull.

Besides, she very rarely went to Melody's house. "I'll call my dad and let him know."

Melody's smile twisted in confusion. "I heard Mom laughing in her room again, too. She's happy. My mother is *never* happy."

The three girls walked the five blocks from school to Melody's home. She lived in a very nice trailer park, where each of the houses had a small front and side yard to plant gardens or flowers. Lace curtains were visible from Melody' windows and the woodwork and stairs were painted a fresh chocolate brown.

They went inside. Rhiannon took a deep breath. "Are those star gazer lilies? I love that smell."

"Yeah. That's Mom's treat to herself on payday at the grocery store. Three stems for ten bucks. Beats air freshener."

"I think they're pretty. My mom doesn't buy flowers, too practical." Bonnie sighed. "She says we can look outside if we want to see them."

Rhee thought about it and shrugged. "My mom prefers plants, so that she can play in the dirt. She loves to work with her hands."

Melody dropped her backpack by the door, took off her coat and slung it over the couch. Bonnie and Rhiannon did the same, then followed Mel into the kitchen.

A round dining table with four chairs sat beneath the window overlooking the side yard. "Sit, guys. Want milk, or root beer? Or water, duh."

"Milk, please," Bonnie said. "So I can dunk. Are we talking chocolate chip cookies?"

"Of course." Melody got down three glasses.

"I'll have milk too," Rhiannon said. "Can I help?"

"I got it." Mel delivered the plate of cookies and the drinks, then sat down. "Thinking about this was all that got me through my last class. Rhiannon, you are way smarter than me. If I'm bored out of my mind, how do you stand it?"

"You are always bored," Bonnie said with a laugh. She broke off a piece of cookie and dunked it in the milk before putting it in her mouth.

"It's a phase," Rhiannon decided, taking a cookie.

"A bored phase?" Melody flipped her hair back. "I want to stick a pencil in my eye. Mrs. Cabernathy's voice just drones on and on and on. I don't care about history. I especially don't care about how she teaches it."

Bonnie nodded empathetically, a cute milk mustache on her upper lip.

"Sticking a pencil in your eye might get you out of class for the day, but then you'd be partially blind for the rest of your life. Not a good solution. When I feel like the classroom walls are closing in and I could scream, I imagine my life as a scientist. Or remember some of the trips I've been on. I make mental notes to self on things I need to do."

"So that's the problem." Melody sighed. "I have nothing I need to do. I don't travel, I'm not rich, I don't have siblings and I don't have a calling."

"Okay, Susie Sunshine!" Rhiannon snorted. "You sure know how to see your glass as half empty."

Bonnie giggled. "That's what makes Mel funny, though. All Gothic."

"You really think I'm negative?" Her brown eyes widened. "I don't think so."

"I am not judging at all," Rhee said carefully. "But you tend to see the darker side of things."

Melody looked to Bonnie, who gave a single nod.

"Oh." Melody dropped half of her cookie to the napkin. "Well." She looked down and Rhee could tell she was trying not to cry.

"Hey, what's the matter?" Rhee asked. Melody was not the kind of girl to get teary eyed over the truth. "You are the first person to stand up for what you believe, and you've made it very clear that you like your shell against the world. That takes an edge. There's nothing wrong with that."

"I told you that I broke it off with Caleb."

"Yeah."

Mel lifted her face, her jaw tight. "Well, he actually broke up with me."

Rhee and Bonnie exchanged a surprised look across the table. "He did?" Rhee wondered why Mel hadn't said so in the first place. Getting dumped meant ice cream and chick flicks with a candy bar chaser.

Melody wiped her eyes. "Uh huh. He said I was too prickly, that he didn't want to have to work so hard to get to know me. Am I that awful?"

Rhiannon's heart broke.

Bonnie leaped up and put her arms around Mel. "You aren't awful at all. He just said that 'cause he's a jerk."

"Did he decide this before or after you wouldn't go all the way?" Rhiannon passed Melody a clean napkin.

"After." Melody sniffed and dabbed at her nose.

"There's your answer. He's a jerk." Rhee shook her head, wishing Caleb was right in front of her so she could put a wart on his nose – or better yet, her fist.

"He's not, really. I guess he thought, I don't know, that I'd be so grateful to have him as a boyfriend," she paused, chewing her trembling lower lip.

"Why?" Rhiannon's desire to help the underdog rose to the fore. "Because he's popular? Hangs out with Jared?"

"He's really cute," Melody said, as if that made everything else okay.

"So?" Rhiannon exhaled. "Being good looking does not give someone the right to be mean. And you are beautiful. Really, really beautiful."

Melody lowered her gaze. "I'm Native American in a small town. Poor, and my dad is in jail."

Rhiannon, sensing the advent of a gigantic pity party, got to her feet. "You have a mom and grandma who love you dearly, a cozy home with plenty to eat. You are pretty, smart and able to speak for yourself." Rhee lifted her shoulder and let it fall. "I mean, I guess if someone labels you a loser, that's one thing. But when you think it of yourself? That's another."

"It's easy for you." Mel refused to look at Rhee, her chin set at a stubborn angle that Rhiannon recognized very well.

Rhee backed up a step. "It is different for me, just like it's different for Bonnie. None of us, even Caleb, have the same journey."

Bonnie rubbed Melody's back. "I wouldn't trade places with Rhiannon. I don't want to see ghosts, and neither do you, Mel, you've always said so."

The three girls sat quietly, absorbing the unusual emotions around them, and sorting through what mattered.

"I'm sorry," Mel said, crumpling her napkin. "I just wish I knew what to do! I sit in that last period of the day, and I want out. I want to leave Crystal Lake and never look back. To go somewhere, a big city, where I can blend in and be judged on me. Not my trailer, or my dad, or my heritage."

"I think it's really cool that you are Kiniwick," Bonnie said in defensive tones. "Your ancestors have been tied to this particular land for hundreds of years. I would want to know everything about it."

"You are welcome to take my place the next time Grandma wants to get together. Always talks about our ancestors. It's like she's trying to make me feel guilty for wanting to leave here."

"Maybe she just wants you to understand. She's verbally passing on what she knows," Rhee suggested. "You should record it. If you don't want to listen to it now, maybe later."

"No thanks."

"Things get forgotten, or lost, in history." Bonnie finished the last of her cookie, leaning against the counter.

"For a reason. It's time to embrace the future." Melody stood and gathered the glasses, carefully scraping the crumbs from the table into her hand, which she dumped in the garbage. "Let's go to my room. I'll show you the letter from my dad."

Rhiannon had a bad feeling as they walked down the narrow carpeted hall. The bathroom was on her right and the two bedrooms followed. First Melody's, and after that, her mom's.

Mel opened the door to her room. Dark navy blue paint was the base color of the interior, with ivory and lighter blue striped wainscoting. A picture window, wide enough for a bench seat, took up one wall and allowed in sunlight. Melody's room had dozens of dream catchers, some with crystals that she'd hung over the window, creating a prism of color along the beige napped carpet.

A small desk and bookshelves ran along the shorter wall, and her full sized bed took the other. It was a comfortable room, and Rhee sat on the bench seat in front of the window.

Bonnie chose the office chair at the desk, and Melody sat cross-legged in the center of her bed.

For the first time Rhiannon really noticed the dream catcher hanging down from the ceiling over Mel's head. Another one was tacked to the wall.

"Tell me about these things. They're really cool. Are they supposed to have crystals?"

Melody shook her head. "Not traditionally. But people like bling, so Grandma sold more, and could make more profit, if she added the crystals."

"I like them, too," Bonnie said, tracing the faint rainbows on the carpet with the toe of her shoe.

"How did you sleep last night, Bonnie?" Rhee asked. "Don't forget that Mel said you could have one of her dream catchers."

"Oh yeah! Take whichever one you want. Grandma gives me a new one each year for my birthday, and on Christmas." She rolled her eyes.

Bonnie tilted her head, the sunlight bouncing off the frames of her glasses. "I slept fine. I did the rose quartz ritual too. It makes me feel good, in here," she tapped her chest.

"Awesome." Rhee smiled. If only there was something like that she could give to Melody. She turned toward her dark haired friend. "You know, you could always try to open yourself up to a little magic."

Mostly joking, knowing very well how Mel felt about it all, Rhiannon was very surprised to get a trickle of chills down her spine, like a drop of ice starting from her nape and rushing down.

"Not gonna happen Rhee."

The dream catcher over Melody's head swung once, then twice, then fell to the bed.

CHAPTER EIGHTEEN

"That was weird." Bonnie took off her glasses and looked from Rhee to Melody.

Melody jumped off the bed, staring up at the ceiling. Fear hovered around her in a tangible beige aura clear enough for Rhiannon to see. "I'm sorry."

"Did you do that?" Melody put her hands on her hips and faced Rhiannon.

"I didn't mean to, if I did." Rhee put her hands up, innocent.

"I'm sure the tack was loose," Bonnie said uncertainly. "But that doesn't explain how it swung back and forth." Bonnie put her glasses back on with a serious expression. "Why would you do that, Rhiannon?"

"I told you, I didn't mean to. I was just sort of kidding around. I think Melody has paranormal abilities, that she ignores."

"So you decided to tear my room apart?" Melody dropped her hands to her sides, mad. Again.

Rhee's brow lifted. "What? The dream catcher dropped, it didn't go flying around your room, like this," Rhiannon lifted the hoop and made it dance before lowering it to the bed.

Bonnie sucked in her lower lip, trying not to laugh. It didn't work and a giggle escaped.

Melody's mouth twitched, and the tension broke as the three of them laughed the scary incident off.

Rhiannon didn't understand the feeling she was getting, but she made sure to touch Melody's arm. "I wouldn't scare you on purpose, okay? I must have been thinking something else, and maybe, I don't know, sometime my abilities escape my control."

"Which is why I want nothing to do with them. The last thing I need is more stuff that can go wrong in my life." Melody gestured around the room. "This is my world, as sucky as it is. I don't need any more crap."

"Back to seeing that half empty glass..." Bonnie pointed out.

"Who's side are you on?" Melody demanded.

"Yours! Always. I just don't want you to be 'bored'. Maybe this," she pointed to the bed and the dream catcher, "is something you need to think about?" Bonnie held out her hands.

Melody scowled. "I'm done talking about this. Okay?"

Typical Melody, getting uncomfortable and closing the door. Rhiannon hadn't thought she'd knocked the dream catcher down – and she certainly hadn't done it on purpose. If she made Mel more upset about it, she'd never relent.

"Fine," Rhee said. "Can we talk about what you might want to do with your grown up self? I assume you don't want to stay in Crystal Lake and be a sixth grade history teacher." Rhiannon kept her tone light, airy and non-confrontational.

Melody smiled. "You got that right. Definitely don't want to be a teacher. Or stay in Crystal Lake."

"What do you like?" Bonnie reached for a piece of paper and a pen from Melody's desk. "We can make a list. I love lists."

Melody was desperate enough to go along with the idea. Rhee sat down, curling her legs beneath her. "How about retail? You are great with the customers who come into Mom's shop."

"There's only a few at a time, so it isn't a big deal." Melody tapped her chin. "And I'm good at taking the online orders and filling them. And balancing the cash register."

"But do you like it?" Bonnie pressed, her pen poised for an answer.

"Yeah. But I wouldn't want to work for someone else. I mean, Mrs. Godfrey's cool, but I've watched some of my mom's boss's and they can be real idiots."

"Oh, so you want to be an entrepreneur?" Rhee asked with a nod.

Bonnie wrote, "Business owner. It's totally doable. So, what business?"

Rhiannon and Bonnie focused on Melody. "I don't know," she said. "This is where I get tempted by the pencil in the eye."

Rhee laughed. "No need. Washington State has all kinds of programs for discounted community college. I'm sure they'd have a certificate program for owning and operating your own business."

"That'd be awesome, Mel!"

"Don't get all excited," Mel said, her eyes flashing. "It takes a ton of money to get businesses off the ground."

"Money is available through grants, especially for minorities." Rhee put her hand over her moonstone pendant, touching the crescent moon for luck.

Melody's face turned red. "I am not using my heritage to get free money!"

"Whoa," Rhee backtracked. "Hang on, Mel. I was talking about being female. Still considered a minority. Don't get my mom started."

"Sorry." Melody exhaled, then looked at Rhee with the glimmer of hope. "Do you really think I could do it? Own my business?"

"Melody, I think you are perfectly suited to do something like that. You are smart, quick, and a hard worker. You aren't afraid to stand up for yourself. Yes."

"I want to save my own money. I don't like the idea of loans." Her brow furrowed. "I have to come up with something, but I will. I mean, I want a car, and now, yeah, I think I want to research that program. It wouldn't be just boring classes, but stuff that pertains to what I'd want to do."

"Nothing boring about that," Rhee said and Bonnie laughed her agreement.

Melody grinned and sat down on the edge of her bed, scooting the dream catcher aside. "That takes the pressure off of running away to Tilton and working at the Burger Barn just to escape."

"That was your plan?" Bonnie giggled.

"What about going to Seattle?" Rhee suggested. "That's just a few hours away. You could still come home for the holidays or summer, but you'd be in a big city."

Melody looked half scared and half exhilarated.

Bonnie's face fell. "I'm all for you finding yourself, but you're leaving me behind."

Melody swallowed and walked across the room to put her hand on Bonnie's shoulder. "We're talking two more years. You'll be tired of me by then."

"I don't think so." She put the paper on the desk. "Just don't forget about me. Us." Bonnie pointed to Rhiannon. "You either." Then, with Bonnie good cheer, she brightened. "I am going to have the best places to vacation for free! Seattle, Las Vegas. Or wherever else you two decide to go."

"It's a deal, Bon-Bon. Friends for life!" Rhee stretched her arms out to the sides. "So now that we have your eyesight protected, do you want to talk about your dad?"

Melody shook her head. "I've had enough touchy feely crap for one day. Wanna watch Friends reruns?"

"Fair enough."

Then, because Melody had been brave enough to look at her true self, Rhee knew she had to do the same. "I can only stay for a while longer."

"Dinner with your folks?" Melody asked.

"No. I have to practice on that stupid bull." Rhee rubbed her aching lower back.

"Think of the kids you're helping," Bonnie said with a sympathetic smile.

"I'm thinking of the hot bath I get to take afterward, and my bed. Janet is going to be the death of me."

CHAPTER NINETEEN

Rhiannon's dad picked her up just in time for dinner.

"I already fed the animals," he said. "How was your visit?"

"Good. I think we got Melody a life goal."

"That's pretty heavy for sixteen."

"No. Not in today's world, Dad. Kids can decide to be on the college tract starting in ninth grade. I knew what I wanted to do from a young age."

"Not everybody is like that. I wandered from career to career until I decided that being an accountant didn't have to mean handcuffed to the computer."

"You are though."

"On my terms. It's different."

Rhiannon felt weighed down. "I'm sort of having one of those what is the point, anyway, kind of days."

"Those are difficult. Unless you know the answer?" Her dad asked in a hopeful tone.

Rhee chuckled. "No. Sorry. What if we never get to find out? What if life is just this giant game of chasing your tail?"

"Your mom insists that life is about the journey. The same thing."

"Ha! Wait until I try to tell her about that."

"Maybe we shouldn't bother her." He gave her a wink.

Rhee and her dad had a different life philosophy than Starla, who innately believed in the good of humanity. She and her dad didn't have that, though they tried. Each was too pragmatic that stuff could and routinely did, go wrong. And yet, her mom was correct, too. Because it always seemed to be okay at the very end.

"It frustrates me," Rhee said, "that Melody refuses to consider her paranormal abilities. I accept her reasons, I understand them, but I can't wait for her to get over it."

Miles tapped the steering wheel with his thumb. "Might not ever happen. There are a lot of people who prefer the paranormal to stay hidden. Why add that element of drama in a calm life?"

"Are you sorry, Dad? That I brought it in?"

"No. It hasn't been easy, but it's been very emotionally rewarding to watch you come into your own. And I get the feeling, from you, that Ashe might be more gifted as well. I expect for you to be a good mentor."

"The best!" Rhee huffed. "As if, Dad." They drove up to their house and Rhiannon realized that while status mattered to Melody, she remained true to her own personality. Rhee knew in her heart that her friend would be okay, whether she accepted her gifts or not.

It could be that Melody used her 'intuition', trusting her gut feelings, and that would be enough.

Dinner, cheese lasagna with a green salad, was just being cleaned up when the house phone rang. "It's Janet," Rhee said with a scowl. "She's going to want to talk about the riding team, and I just don't want to."

"You could have said no," her dad said.

"You still can," her mom reminded her.

"I can't either." The phone stopped ringing and the machine picked up. Janet left a message, asking Rhee to call her back as soon as possible.

"Well?" Starla asked. "Are you going to?"

"Later. She makes my stomach ache. I looked over the profiles of the other girls, and they seem like good candidates for the team. Young."

Her dad laughed. "Because you are so old."

Rhee rolled her eyes. "Inexperienced?"

He shrugged his shoulders, not willing to argue.

"Well. I guess I better go practice." Her back ached, her legs ached, and the last thing she wanted to do was go out to the barn and ride that bull. She'd promised.

Her mom gave her a sympathetic laugh. "A half hour, and I'll put some lavender salts in your bath. You are being very good about this. Do you want me to call Janet for you?"

"No, thanks. I can make my own phone calls." Rhee giggled. "Do you remember when Jared's mom broke up with me over the phone?"

Her dad stood, arms crossed. "That family. I cannot begin to understand them."

Starla got their coats so they could trek out to the barn together. "Might as well get it over with."

"Did you go to the shop at all today?" Rhee asked.

"No. Kept it locked tight." Starla zipped up the front of her heavy wool jacket.

"I tried to peek in the windows, but I didn't see anything out of the ordinary," her dad said, putting on some thin leather gloves.

Rhee, because she needed to have freedom of movement, wore a thick sweat jacket. She'd be hot enough within five minutes of the bull to not need anything but a tee shirt.

"Dr. Richards hasn't sent me any information. Maybe by the time we're done here tonight?"

"I have to open the shop on Saturday," her mom said. "I can't really wait any longer than that."

"I know. Dad will have to be with you because I've got this thing."

"It will all be fine." Her mom smiled. Rhee exchanged a quick glance with her dad. Her mom always thought things would be fine.

The shop was in the opposite direction of the barn, but when Rhee put out psychic feelers, she didn't get anything from Celestial Beginnings. Of course, she hadn't ever, anyway. Whatever the Oneiroi statues were, they had to be incredibly powerful to keep shielded.

Forty five minutes later, the trio trudged back to the house. Rhee was soaked from scalp to sole. "I just want a bath."

Her dad grinned. "You were getting into it. I think it's coming back to you. You didn't fall half as much as you did yesterday."

Clapping her hands, her mom said, "You looked like you were one with the bull. It's beautiful, in an odd way. You have to be agile. I couldn't do it. Without practice."

Rhee gave her mom a horrified look. "Stay off the bull."

"It will be a great way to get my figure back after Ashe is born."

Miles briefly closed his eyes and muttered something that sounded like Goddess Help Me.

Rhee snickered and followed them back inside the house. Thor meowed and Rhee looked at the answering machine. Three messages? She hit play. Janet's message. Ugh.

Dr. Richards, asking her to call him back.

And J.W..

The man's voice sounded vibrant, full of life and joy. "Sorry to have missed your call, Rhiannon. I wish I could be of more help. The Oneiroi came to me via an anonymous donor. I believe the statues to be haunted. Because Morpheus is supposed to be a dream messenger, I went to sleep asking where I should send them on my retirement. All three nights, your name came to mind. So, I wrapped them up – bubble wrap and packing tape seem to keep them quiet – and sent them off. I am entering the Rain Forest, so I will be out of touch for some time. Heard a rumor there's a crystal cave with healing properties somewhere inside. Wish me luck, as I do for you. The Oneiroi are mischievous, but not harmful, to my knowledge. But watch the fanged one. I don't trust him."

"Wow." Rhee looked at her parents. "That's all great information, but nothing we hadn't already guessed."

"Nothing that's going to help me open my store Saturday," her mom said, crossing her arms.

"I will run into town tomorrow and load up on bubble wrap. Packing tape. We'll catch those little demons, Rhiannon, if we have to tear down every last shelf."

Rhee exhaled. Her dad was not messing around. "Pick me up after school. We can start as soon as I get home."

"Are we sure that's a good idea?" Her mom narrowed her eyes. "I don't want you hurt. I think we need to do a protection spell before we go inside the shop."

"You are not coming," Miles said, his expression determined.

"I,"

"You are pregnant. You are going to stay here, inside the house, where it is safe. These things attacked Rhiannon, drawing blood with stuffed animals." He stared at Starla until she gave a slow nod, her turn to compromise.

"Fine. But you are both going to be protected before you go. Or else we can burn down the barn, and the demons with it."

CHAPTER TWENTY ONE

Her mother's extreme suggestion persuaded Rhiannon that doing the magic circle before entering the shop was the right plan of action.

After avoiding both twins all day, she'd managed to make it to car line and her dad without having a confrontation. Honestly, she wasn't up to listening to Janet's grating voice.

Instead, she'd texted back and forth with Tanya on the subject of demons. Tanya told her that the Greeks did not separate demons into good and evil – that came later, with church dogma. That they were quasi-divine beings acting as invisible voices, some thought between the gods and men. Not sure how that helped, but it was interesting.

"To the north, to the east, the south and west." Starla guided the candle ritual. Dressed in white, as were her parents, Rhee absorbed the magick of love and added its power to her psychic shield. "Earth. Air. Fire. Water." Each element was represented at the altar, and within the circle.

Her mother's eyes were closed as she bowed her head and prayed for protection. "For Rhiannon, my daughter. Brave healer of the spiritually wounded. For Miles, my husband, warrior, protector. Guide them, keep them safe in the light of the Lord and the Lady as they face mischievous spirits. Dream demons, be gone. So mote it be."

They waited for the white candle to burn down before closing the circle, spending the time in quiet reflection before what could be a battle.

When it was over, Starla placed a large hunk of hematite in each of their palms. "Visualizing the shields will work best, but having the added protection of the hematite will aid in grounding yourselves, if you feel overwhelmed."

"Thanks, Mom. Dad." Rhee headed for the stairs. "I'm changing into jeans, first, then we can go."

It took less than ten minutes to put on comfortable clothes and twist her hair into a knot she clipped at her nape. She slipped the hematite in her front jeans pocket, wore her moonstone necklace, and long sleeves. At the last second she grabbed thin leather gloves, in case she was attacked again by flying purple kittens.

Her dad waited, similarly attired. "Ready to bag us some dream demons?"

"Very redneck, Dad. Nice." She led the way out the back and outside toward the shop.

When they reached the door, Rhiannon used her telepathic skills to unlock and open it. The various scents of candles and oils rushed toward them in an overpowering wave.

"They must have gotten bored," Rhiannon said, cautiously stepping over the threshold, searching for anything out of place.

"Your mother won't be happy if they've destroyed the inside. We need her happy."

"I know." Rhiannon turned on the lights, one at a time. Uncertain as to what to expect, she exhaled with relief. "Not as bad as that first time, when we called Officer Julianne." She eyed the stacked tower of couch cushions and the precariously balanced candles reaching from the floor to the ceiling. "More creative though."

She felt her dad's apprehension as he followed her inside the shop. "What are they trying to say?"

"Once I figure that out then I'll know what to do with them." She scanned the room, then pointed to the fallen stuffed kittens around the floor. "They aren't very good at putting their toys away."

"Should we clean up?"

Rhiannon decided to take a proactive stand. "First, let's have tea."

Her dad arched his black brow, but headed toward the long counter. "Any Earl Gray?"

"You bet." Rhiannon felt invisible eyes on her as she got down two mugs from the cupboard. The tea canister moved an inch just as she reached for it.

"Hello there," she said, alert while acting nonchalant.

"Did that just move?"

"Yup."

"I'll take two honey."

Rhee smiled over her shoulder at her dad, who sat on a stool and propped his elbows on the counter. She discreetly glanced around the room to see if the Oneiroi would pop up anywhere, but so far, nothing. "You aren't afraid of a sugar rush?"

"I have a feeling I'll need my energy."

She turned and brought the tea to her dad, whispering, "Keep your hematite in your pocket. I am too."

He nodded and brought the steaming mug to his nose. "This reminds me of my childhood. My father always drank Earl Gray tea on the weekends, while he read the paper. You would have loved your Grandpa."

"If he was anything like you, Dad, then duh." She sat and enjoyed her lemon zest, just two people ignoring the chaos to have tea.

The spirits, wanting to be acknowledged, didn't like their lack of reaction. The cushions fell sideways, landing in a heap on the floor.

"If those candles break," her dad muttered.

"It will be a mess." Rhee shrugged, not wanting to give the spirit any emotion. "No big deal. We can't reach the top of that tower, anyway."

A rush of air waved over Rhiannon's shoulder. *It had been that close?*

Like a tiny cyclone, air swirled around the highest candle, bringing it down and setting it on the floor. Rhee and her dad watched from the corner of their eyes, not giving the entity their full on attention. The last candle set on the floor completed the shape of a heart.

"That is sweet," Rhee said softly.

Two hot gusts of energy twisted around her before darting through the center of the shape, breaking it apart.

"Jealous spirits?" Her dad suggested in cool tones. "Maybe one of them has a crush on you."

"And the other two don't like it. Could explain the angry behavior." She took a thoughtful sip. "We need to find the statues."

"That's the plan. Any specific ideas on how?"

Rhee frowned, raising her voice but still speaking in conversational tones. "I read that Morpheus is the leader of the Oneiroi." A blast of heat made her eyes water. "He can speak as a mortal man in the dreamer's dreams."

Shielded from true harm, Rhiannon pressed the tangent. "And that Phobetor, a lesser dream god, can only appear as a monster." The cupboard rattled behind her, but she showed no outer concern.

Her dad's hand tightened around the mug, but he too, kept cool.

"Phantasos is nothing. Inanimate objects? I think I feel sorry for him, really."

A gust of wind as powerful as a tornado cycled the stuffed kittens up from the floor in a spinning motion, going faster and faster and faster before erupting toward the ceiling. They fell heavily.

"Raining cats and cats," Rhiannon said.

"I think we know who that last one is," her dad observed. "Does that help you in any way?"

"If they are the true Oneiroi, then yes. We know who they are." Rhee paused, tracing her finger along the rim of the mug. "Now to find out what they want."

"You?"

"Not so easy, I don't think." Rhiannon thought hard, trying to come up with a plan to find the spirit's statues. "Maybe they just want a place to stay for a while."

Her mug was pushed from her hands so hard it slid off the counter and broke on the wooden floor. Tea splashed and lemon zest filled the air.

"Or not," her dad commented dryly.

Rhee lifted her eyes, meeting his gaze. "I sense that one of the spirits is stronger than the others. Frustrated. They aren't working together, but one is in direct opposition of the other two."

She had no clear reasons for this, no visions or images, but relied on her intuition. Feelings.

"Did a priestess bind your spirits to the statues? Is that why you are angry – it has been over two thousand years." Rhee tapped the counter. "What did you do that was so terrible?"

Rhiannon left the counter and walked across the floor, lightly kicking the stuffed kittens to one side. "I haven't read anything about the three of you, brothers, doing anything so rotten you deserved banishment."

She felt the air warming, a soft caress over her face. Taking a deep breath she said, "But I'm sure you deserved it."

The air turned hot and the couch tipped over, knocking aside the basket of quilts. "Tell me, if I'm wrong. How can I help you? Show me the statues."

The blankets and knick knacks fell from the high shelves, the fragrant oils shattering on the wood floor.

"You cross the line between mischief and destruction. Is this why you are bound? Justifiably banished." Rhee held out her arms, catching the last of the oils in an energy net before any more could break.

"You didn't know I could do that, I sense your surprise." She bowed her head, sorting through the various levels of vibration. They were more than surprised. Pleased?

She telepathically gathered the kittens, floating them back to the counter, and the wicker basket. She straightened the couch, folded the blankets. "Do not mess with me, or mine. I am not afraid of you. I am powerful enough to help you."

Air so hot it made her cough rushed her face like getting too close to a flame, blowing her hair back as if caught in a raging wind.

"Let me help you."

Witch. Dream Witch Dreamer Witch. Dream. Just wait until you dream, witch. Dream.

CHAPTER TWENTY TWO

Rhiannon's show of strength angered the demons, and made her one exhausted cookie.

Her dad helped her back to the house, each holding their hematite in their palms. The spirits had slammed the door at their backs.

"That went well," he said, holding her elbow. "Taunting them to make them angry. Showing off your powers. They didn't bring out the statues, and they promised to give you nightmares." He shook his head. "Was that really the plan?"

Rhee opened the back door. "We were on a quest for knowledge. We learned that there are really three separate spirits and not just one."

"Scarier, actually."

She shrugged. "Better to know what I'm up against."

"You're back!" Starla came around the corner from the stairs to the hall. "I thought you would be gone longer."

"It seems Rhee has a gift for making the demons mad. It might a teenager thing. There are times..."

"Miles." Starla shook her head before taking Rhee's hand. "I've set out your bath. Basil and clove for added protection, rock salt. Make the water nice and hot."

"I should call Dr. Richards." The idea of a warm, cleansing bath lured her away from the phone and up the stairs to the bathroom.

"He called while you were over there. You can do it after the bath, Rhee. You have dark circles under your eyes. The candles are lit, all you have to do is add the water."

Her mom gave her a little push up the stairs.

"Okay." What had she learned tonight, that she could concretely share with Tanya and Dr. Richards? Three spirits, not in accord. *Dream, witch.*

She drew the bath and got in the tub, sinking back to allow the water to her neck, where it tickled the base of her chin. Warmth started from her toes, traveling upward like a healing balm. The herbs and oils smelled clean, fresh and the rock salt ensured purification of both spirit and flesh. The candles flickered in the steamy mirror, creating a calming atmosphere where her mind wandered.

Three spirits. After addressing them today, she was fairly certain that each spirit was that of the Oneiroi. How long had they been trapped in the marble statues? Tales of the gods had been around since 400 BC, or earlier, but the statues dated 200 AD. From what she remembered of Greek history, temples were common, and cults formed around certain gods. She could ask Dr. Richards about that. His stories were better than Google.

Water steamed, fogging the mirror. Her eyelids drooped as she relaxed into the hot water.

She'd read that Morpheus had a love interest. Iris, the rainbow. Iris delivered a message from the head honcho – Hypnos, who was possibly Morpheus' father. Iris married another, perhaps breaking Morpheus' heart? Love, drama, comedy, tragedy. Some things were the same throughout time.

Love made her think of Dane. Of Bonnie and Corey. Would they make it together? She figured Tanya and Matthew would stay friends, but move on. Caleb, and Felicity. Finished.

Could Morpheus have a crush on her? Rhee wiggled her pink toes. If he'd been cognizant of her from television, or J.W. talking about her, she supposed it was possible.

How to get the spirits to willingly go back to their statues, where she could capture them?

"And what then, Rhee?" She asked the question aloud, vocals reverberating across the sauna like room. "Now that I know who they are, I can bind them, or tighten the binding spell already on them. Once I have them trapped, I can address them and decide what to do."

Mind clear and pointed in a single direction instead of many different paths, Rhee soaked until the water cooled. She got out, wrapping herself in an absorbent lavender scented towel, choosing a smaller towel for her hair. When she looked up at the fogged mirror, her sense of serenity evaporated.

An invisible finger traced the words, *Dream Witch Dreamer Witch.*

Mouth dry, Rhee leaned forward and wiped them away as if they didn't exist. Perhaps the Oneiroi's powers weren't confined to the shop as she'd thought.

She decided not to share that information with her mom, knowing it would unnecessarily freak her out. "Get back to your statue and stay away from this house, this is my sacred space, demon. Be gone!"

Rhiannon's eyes seemed heavier and heavier and she left the bathroom, steam escaping behind her like a scented cloud.

Up the stairs, each leg weighing a thousand pounds, each step feeling like she'd dragged it through quicksand. She opened her bedroom door, slipped into flannel pajamas and kept the towel wrapped around her wet hair. She lay on her bed, just to rest her eyes for a minute, no more than that, she assured herself. Cold, she got under the covers. To stop the chill, not to sleep. It was too early to go to bed. She had to call Dr. Richards.

Rest.

Just for minute.

The air, hot and dry, the desert sand scraping particles across his skin. Thirsty, by Zeus, water or wine would quench his thirst. His parched throat.

The mountains behind grew larger instead of smaller as he ran away from his master. Away from his cane, his knotted rope, his brutal punishments for minor infractions.

When Hypnos realized what he'd done, forgiveness might not be forthcoming no matter how many lashes doled out. Three winged marble figurines, securely tied in his pack, belonged to him now. Morpheus, Phobetor, and Phantasos. Three brothers, quasi gods, who could foretell fortunes to the dreamer. He would control them all. He, the acolyte, would create his own fortune. He'd broken the dream wand, for good measure.

CHAPTER TWENTY THREE

Despite falling asleep by seven last night, Rhiannon snored right through her alarm and was late for school.

"Are you getting sick?" Her mom handed over a piece of peanut butter toast. "Maybe you should stay home."

Rhee shook her muzzy head. "I can't miss any school, remember?" Principal McGavin had made it quite clear that there would be no more special privileges for Rhiannon throughout the year – it caused problems for the other students.

She supposed it was fair, but as she climbed the stairs to school, bed sounded so much better.

She dozed through class, and slid onto the lunch bench in the cafeteria, barely able to concentrate.

"Didn't sleep last night?" Bonnie asked, pushing over a few apple slices. Rhee was too tired to go get food.

"You having bad dreams too?" Melody leaned on the table. "That's it. You both need dream catchers."

"It wasn't a bad dream – I dreamed about those stupid statues. Some servant guy stole them, thinking he'd be rich but instead he must have earned himself some bad karma."

"Stealing could do it," Melody agreed. "One of the Do Not rules."

"I want a new dream catcher, Mel. I know you know how to make them. I want a green one. Rhee wants a blue one. Can we have crystals?"

"I called my grandma yesterday, she told me how to do a simple one. You seemed so freaked out about using one of mine that I figured I'd see how it worked."

"Well?" Rhiannon prodded, impressed that Melody had taken her day of self-discovery so far.

"I can tie a knot," she said with a mysterious smile.

"Yeah!" Bonnie looked at Rhee. "See, Melody will make you your own to catch the bad guy in your dream. I mean, the slave guy is bad, right?"

"I can't remember how it ends. Even that much is fuzzy, compared to the actual dream." She rubbed her forehead.

"Hey!" Janet's voice came up behind her, startling Rhee into falling off her elbow. She turned around and glared.

"What?"

"I called you. It is customary to return phone calls when people ask you to. Unless they don't teach you that at psycho school?" She put her hand on her hip, looking perfect in jeans and a fitted flannel shirt.

"Sorry." Rhee lifted her head, realizing she'd thrown on a black tee shirt that wasn't at all cute. "I am exhausted."

"Practicing the bull?" Janet's green eyes glittered.

Because it was easier to admit the truth than come up with a witty, snarky comment, Rhiannon nodded. "Yeah. It's kicking my butt."

Janet crossed her arms, studying Rhiannon. "You look awful."

"Thanks for the confirmation of how I feel." She exhaled. "What did you want?"

"It can wait." Janet left the group with a finger wave that mostly consisted of her middle finger.

Bonnie made a frustrated noise. "I wish you wouldn't help her."

"At this particular moment, I couldn't agree more, Bon."

Corey sang about losing that loving feeling. Rhee dropped her head back to her folded arms, adding, "Oh, oh, oh."

Melody laughed and slapped the table, in a rare good mood.

"Seriously, Rhiannon, don't give up your day jobs," Corey teased.

"Something you haven't aced," Melody noted. "The scales."

"You guys are kicking me while I'm down," she mumbled, wishing she could lift her head and fight back. Or at least eat some more of that apple slice. She was thirsty, like the slave or servant in the dream. She felt like she could sleep for a week.

Bonnie patted her back. "Forget the bull for tonight. Go home and take a nap." She added, "You'll need the sleep. Dane's coming tomorrow!"

Bone tired, Rhee couldn't even summon up the enthusiasm to smile. Considering how much she missed her boyfriend, that said a lot about her mental state.

Once the terribly long day finally ended, Rhiannon got into her dad's car half asleep.

Concerned, he touched her forehead. "You don't feel hot, but you look awful."

"I'm not sick." She didn't think so, anyway. "Tired. I'm so freaking tired."

"Dr. Richards called, he left a message in response to your message. He said that cults were very common, and he couldn't find any more information about Iris pertaining to Morpheus. I hope that makes sense, because I don't understand."

Her dad turned out of the school parking lot to the street.

"I understand, but it wasn't helpful. I was sort of hoping that Morpheus, the spirit who formed a heart with the candles, could be linked to Iris. I don't know why. Just following a thought."

"We need proof," Miles said with a commiserating smile.

"Sometimes I wish it was easier for me to just act on faith, like Mom."

"Well, instead of discounting your theory completely, set it to the back of your mind and move on to the next one. Which would be?"

"That's all I had." She expelled a breath. "No, the cult and the temples. The acolyte in my dream."

"Dr. Richards asked if you'd been keeping a dream journal?"

"No. I rarely dream important stuff! This is unusual."

"So write it down," her dad suggested. "It won't be too late once we get home."

"I have to do the bull tonight. I missed last night."

"You were so tired we couldn't even wake you for dinner. And for you to miss dinner?" He elbowed her and smiled.

"I know I should be hungry, but I'm just," she searched for the best word, "lethargic. Walking through wet cement."

"Nice." Her dad turned into their driveway. "Your mom has made a feast to make up for missed meals, so it would be good if you did more than nibble, all right?"

"Got it."

"No bucking machine unless you eat. I won't let you risk your neck. Being this wiped won't help you hang on, and I won't risk the pads not being enough. You've got to be alert."

"Okay. I understand. You are in Super Dad mode." She went into the kitchen and forced herself to eat some soup, which made her feel better immediately. Not one hundred percent, but fifty percent was pretty awesome after zero.

"A biscuit?" Starla passed the bread basket.

"You're the best," Rhee said, taking small pieces but eating it all.

"What's the plan?" Her mom sat at the table. "Because I have an idea. I know you don't want to talk about Dream Divination, but,"

Rhee opened her mind and made herself listen. "I'm ready. Give it to me."

"The moon goddess, who you are named for, is adept at reading dreams." Starla was so excited her bracelets chimed as she clapped her hands. "I think if we cram, like you would for a test last minute, you might be able to absorb enough to ask this Morpheus to speak to you in a dream."

Rhee, halfway tuning her mom and the moon goddess out, jerked her head up, instantly awake. "What did you say?"

"I know! See Miles, I told you this would be a good idea," her mom said with a laugh. "The moon goddess can help you lure that dream demon into your dream. You can ask him what he wants from you. But you have to prepare, first. I can help!"

"Well, Rhee?" her dad asked, tapping the table between them to gain her attention. "What do you think?"

Dream, witch. Hadn't he told her what to do, too? Energized, she said, "I like it. I think it could totally work." Her mind turned over one scenario after the other. "Isn't that what J.W. did? Ask for the answer to come in his dream?"

"It took three nights," her mom reminded her.

"At least then I'd have a better idea of what to do with the spirits. They can't keep behaving like spiritual felons, with the malicious mischief."

"I pulled all sorts of articles from the internet and printed out the best ones. Just to give you a crash course."

"Thanks Mom." Rhiannon began to feel a little more like her regular self. "Can I have another bowl of soup?"

"And another biscuit?" Starla pushed the basket toward her.

Thor meowed from his place over the sink.

"He must be hungry too."

"Dad, you know how hard it is to watch over us all. He's helping."

"He does a great job," her mom said. "Miles, do you want a bowl, too? It's cold in the barn, if you are planning on being with Rhee while she practices."

Her dad accepted some soup. Rhee realized her mom just wanted to make sure her family was cared for, nurtured. Loved. "Don't forget that Dane will be here for dinner tomorrow night."

"I haven't. I'm trying to decide on the menu."

"He likes everything."

"That actually makes things more complicated." Starla sighed. "Sometimes it's better to start with what you don't want and work back from there."

Rhee perked up, her senses alert. "Mom, I think you might be onto something."

CHAPTER TWENTY FOUR

She pushed the bowl aside and grabbed paper and pen for a list. Her thoughts jumbled together, and she had to sort them out so she could think.

"What do we know? What don't we know?"

Her dad ate and shook his head. "I think you are better off writing down what you remembered about your dream."

"The first night, you didn't dream anything, right?" Starla asked.

"Right. But I'm pretty sure I dreamed of Greece for that short time after I fainted."

"Were you a part of the dream, or watching from above?"

"I barely remember," Rhee said, putting the end of the pen to her lower lip. So she didn't forget, she added her questions at the top of the page, then flipped to a fresh page for the dream stuff. It was like eating her mom's soup banished a foggy mind spell.

"Time to carry a notepad for a while," her mom suggested. "What did you feel after the couch dream?"

"Angry. Mad." She closed her eyes, reaching back into her memory. "I remember a lake, and trees. Maybe there was a cave?"

"Where were you?" Her dad's question, the bones, her mom's question, the emotion.

"Watching, definitely watching. And I guess I must not have been able to do anything about what was happening. That would have made me mad for sure." Rhiannon opened her eyes, blinking until she could focus. "Even if I didn't know what was happening. I felt deceived. Last night I dreamed and, man, it was totally different than the norm for me."

"Honey, you were so tired, I wish you could have stayed home today and slept. But it made me wonder if Morpheus is trying to get you to sleep, so he can talk to you in your dreams?"

Rhiannon shivered. "That's creepy Mom. That some old Greek dream demon could exert that much power, from so far away? And besides, his power should only be able to affect me at night!"

"You don't know the rules, right, Rhiannon?" Her dad's gentle reminder hit home.

"Right. Right. I don't know, so I should stop trying to make these entities fit my perimeters." She groaned. "It's so hard."

"You can do it." Miles nodded with assurance.

Starla pointed to the paper. "Last night's dream. You say it was different. Were you the same person in the dream?"

"That's ridiculous, I," she sighed with frustration. "I don't know." She stood, dropping the pen to the table. "I think riding the bull is a good idea. I need to break out of this funk. It feels like being wrapped in a too tight blanket and my mind is a polluted, heavy fog."

"All right," Miles rose too, grabbing two apples from the fruit basket in the center of the table. "Let's go wake you up."

Thor followed them out to the barn, patrolling the way, it seemed. "Makes me wonder what he thinks about the spirits. Do some bother him, and others don't? From what Mom said about the statues when they made the mess inside the shop, Thor was crazy mad."

"And he didn't like Suzanne, either." Her dad stopped by Moonstone and fed her an apple. Betsy got a petunia bought from the Home Depot until Starla could grow them come spring.

"Yeah, but Suzanne teased him." She acknowledged the hint of sadness that the memory brought. "Sometimes I miss her."

"If she hadn't been coerced into bad magic, she would have been a good contact for you as a medium in the spirit world. She was one of your first friends, and your first ghost."

Surprised by her dad's understanding, Rhee sighed. "Mrs. Edwards has much more power than I do."

"You're sixteen," her dad said with a laugh. "I was thinking, Rhiannon, what if, like Suzanne, the entities attached to the statues can be controlled?"

Rhiannon put on her helmet and pads as her dad turned on the machine. The mechanical humming made the floorboards rumble. She stretched her sore muscles, leaning over to touch her toes, then reaching up toward the ceiling of the barn. She noticed the neatly repaired patch in the far corner.

"Hey! Nice job, Dad."

"Your mom convinced me to hire a handy man. She said she didn't have the energy to take me to the hospital." He looked disgruntled, but then laughed. "I agreed. Right now, what your mom wants she can have. But once Ashe is born? I might even buy a tool belt."

Rhee snorted. "Watch out, world! It's good to have a hobby."

"It's called farm maintenance. Work."

"Work that makes you happy, just like catching spirits makes me happy."

"Forget happy for the next hour. You, Rhee, are going to be miserable." He grinned and flipped on the accelerator.

Rhee had no time to think about demi gods or dreams as she gripped the handle of the bull and held on, or fell off, accordingly. As she fell the last time, landing on a mat and staring up at the ceiling with Thor staring down at her from the wooden stall ledge, she gasped, "What time did I get?"

Her dad handed her a bottle of water. "Still not where you were. You're older though."

"A year is not going to slow me down!"

"We have tomorrow afternoon to practice, but even if you were to go now, you would qualify." He helped her up.

"Thanks. That is all I need. Nothing fancy."

"Your competitive nature has yet to fully take over."

She wiped her sweaty face with a towel. "Dane can't wait to see me do this. It's the last thing I think he should see. Me, gross and sweaty."

"Dane will get a kick out of it. He's a good kid, Rhee. How's it going for you two, with him being in another state?"

"I really missed him last weekend, but it isn't different from when he lived in Tilton. I went to school during the week, and he would come over on the weekends. We Skype, and text." She nodded and admitted, "I can't think about him with other girls, because then I'd be jealous. I have to trust that he wants to be with me, like I do with him."

"That is a very mature attitude."

"Well," Rhee joked, "I am a prodigy."

"As if I could ever forget?"

After bedding down the animals, she and her dad walked back to the house. Her mom had a dozen books on the table, and a few articles printed out.

"Edgar Cayce was the best documented dream diviner in history. He could lay back, close his eyes, and answer any question posed to him. I think he may have had the ability to travel out of body."

Rhee read the dates on the books. "1930, 1935. Can't you find anybody from the 21st century?"

"If it ain't broken," her mom drawled, "why fix it?"

"Good point. But Mom, I don't want to tell the future, I just want to figure out what the dream means."

"I know! I'm trying to give you options here. See, I have a few from Swami Radha, the Practice of Dream Yoga."

"No yoga, thanks, Mom." She exhaled. "Sheesh! How many dream dictionaries are there?"

"A lot. The most important thing though are symbols, and you can really create your own key to dream divination." Starla spread the information out. "There are steps to make dream analysis easier for the beginner. You've already started by writing your dream down."

She rifled through the piles and came up with a list. "Write it down, study it for words that resonate."

Rhee plunked down into a chair. "I appreciate all of this, Mom, I really do. But I think I'd like a cup of chamomile tea, one of the cookies you made the other day, and a good book. I promise to write down any dreams as soon as I wake up in the morning."

Her mom frowned. "But,"

"You've shown me the important stuff, but my brain is on overload."

Her dad put his hand on her shoulder and gave it a squeeze. "Your plan sounds like a good one. Not to add any pressure to a situation out of our immediate control, but if we can't clear the spirits from the shop, your mom won't be able to open on Saturday. We need to prepare."

Rhee breathed in, searching for calm. "I'm trying."

"I know." Starla stood and gathered the things together in a stack. "You know what? Don't worry about Saturday. I'll put a note up on the website that Celestial Beginnings is closed for renovations. I'll find paperwork or something for Melody to do from the house."

Gratitude warmed Rhee from the inside out. "Are you sure? I hate for you to miss out on business. Those church ladies love to come in and have tea."

"They can wait until next week, when I give them a fifty percent off coupon for the inconvenience." Starla tapped the table and smiled. "I don't want you rushing to banish those dream demons until you have a better idea on how to do it."

"Thanks." Relieved of one stress point, Rhiannon paused as a title from the stack caught her attention. "Selene. Greek Moon Goddess." Tugging the book from the pile, she headed to the cupboard for a mug. "This looks like the perfect book for a little light reading."

CHAPTER TWENTY FIVE

Rhee took the book, the cookies and the tea upstairs to her room. Moon rays lit a path of silver across her floor, and she curled up in the chair by the window, setting the tea on the window's ledge. Thor coiled next to the plate, staring outside at the tree's shadows.

She'd traveled, been in new homes and fancy hotels, but this old farmhouse had heart, love and warmth. Despite all obstacles, it was a safe haven against the world. She nibbled the edge of a cookie and opened the thin volume on Selene, her namesake.

"Okay. Greek mythology. Robed goddess, hmm. Crescent moon as a symbol. Got that covered." She tapped her moonstone pendant with the silver crescent moon. "Ha! The bull is a symbol for Selene too. Wait 'til I tell Dad in the morning."

She'd studied a little bit about the moon goddess after embracing her path toward faith, along with science. But there was only so much time in the day, and other things took priority.

Honestly, dream divination simply didn't capture her interest. Like her mom said, it was symbols and interpretation, and it would be different for everybody.

"I got other stuff on my plate," she told Thor, who agreed with a loud purr.

Rhiannon continued to read, her eyes getting heavier and heavier. By the time she'd finished her tea and cookies, she was warm, full and ready for bed.

Teeth brushed, face washed, jammies on, Rhee crawled beneath the covers, Thor rumbling good night as he stretched against her back.

Her last thought as she went to sleep was a prayer for open mindedness, and that she would dream something helpful for demon spirits. It required being vulnerable, which she didn't particularly like, but if Morpheus had something to say – she wanted to hear it.

On the edge of sleep, Dream Rhiannon spread out her arms, realizing she wore a silver robe that draped over her shoulders in a silken fall to the floor. Open in the front, a dazzling crystal gown peeped through the lapels.

Rhee wiggled her bare toes. Neither warm nor cold, she looked around, seeing a set of winged white horses and a silver chariot and knowing they belonged to her. She sat on a white throne of ivory, carved with embossed bulls. If she looked down, her gaze followed a path of moonlight leading to the world below. She adjusted her sight by narrowing her gaze, bringing into focus people, houses, and individuals tucked cozily in their beds.

A sense of wellbeing filled her. She blessed those she passed and time shifted, going back, back and back over a thousand years.

Where was she? Even in her dream state, Rhiannon was very aware that she and the Goddess Selene were one. Ancient Greece, a thin peninsula, finally a large white temple that felt like home.

The goddess did not speak to her, but showed her the world as she saw it. Long haired women in sleeveless white tunics and silver circlets served the temple. A woman's goddess, Rhee realized the prayers to Selene centered around night magic, children, and love.

Rhee wondered if the prayers were ever answered, but received no reply from her hostess.

They traveled the city, and Rhiannon noticed many temples and prayer sites, all dedicated to different gods. They stopped next at the temple to Morpheus and the Oneiroi.

Here the people prayed to Morpheus for answers to everyday problems, for guidance through dreams. Symbols of the dream gate, and the dream wand, were etched on the columns outside the temple. Winged demons, two horrific, one fair, were in bas relief on the door. Morpheus, good looking, had the gift of appearing as a human in dreams.

Phobetor, bringer of monsters in the form of animals. Phantasos, creator of fantastical nightmares.

Thousands of years later, humanity still searched for truth, for hints of what was to come, Rhee thought. Were the answers elusive on purpose? Before she could hold on to the thought, it flew away, just as Selene took her to the temple for Zeus.

Selene reigned during the popular times of Morpheus, of the Oneiroi. Rhiannon remembered reading that Zeus had granted Selene a wish, to keep her human lover young by gifting, through Hypnos, eternal sleep. Hypnos was the father of Morpheus, Phobetor and Phantasos.

Did Selene, Moon Goddess, fight for popularity among the other quasi gods? For recognition? Maybe there were only so many alms to go around, and the minor deities had to duke it out for a top position in the hearts of the people.

Before Rhee could explore that thought further, they flew without effort over homes, through time, to return to Selene's throne. Security reigned as Rhiannon-Selene overlooked her domain.

Rhiannon's alarm blared, bringing her abruptly from her dream.

Thor cocked his ear forward, grumpy. He knew they should have another thirty minutes of sleep, and he wasn't happy about the early wake up call.

"Sorry," Rhee giggled and kissed his nose. "I have to write the dream details down." She leaned over and picked up her pen and paper, telepathically flipping on the light switch so she could see what she scribbled.

Already the images evaporated, as if chased by dawn.

"I was seeing through the goddess's eyes, which was pretty freaking cool." Writing down what she remembered helped formulate thought to word. She didn't bother trying to do it all in order, she didn't want to lose anything that might be important later.

Her mom knocked on the door a half later, carrying a cup of strong black tea and a bagel with cream cheese.

Rhee looked up, blinking Starla into focus. Her mom wore a flowing skirt and three quarter length sleeve tee. Not a toga or a tunic. She'd been so ensconced in her memories of ancient Greece she'd completely lost track of time.

"Morning!" Starla brought the tray to the bed, and sat down, barely missing Rhee's feet. "I knew you were awake. I could feel it." She pointed to the tablet of paper. "I guess you had a good dream? Lots of details? Morpheus?"

"No demons. Selene would have been worshipped in ancient Greece, right? Had her own temple and everything?"

"Sure," Starla agreed.

"Well, what if the Oneiroi had a temple, too? And they overlapped or competed or something?" She couldn't shake the idea that Selene and Morpheus had a connection.

"Interesting." Starla took a sip of Rhee's tea before trading the pad for the mug. "Breakfast. While you are at school today, I'll cross reference them all and see what happens."

That felt right, Rhee realized, taking a drink. "Hot!" She frowned, then reached for the bagel, biting the crispy edge. "Maybe I can fix this in time for you to open in the morning."

"Don't even worry about. I've already posted the notice that we're closed. If people really want one of my scented pillows, they can order it on line. Take your time."

She couldn't explain why, but Rhiannon felt the need to hurry. "I don't think we should delay."

"What else can we do?" Starla rose from the bed, setting the tablet on the nightstand. "Rhiannon, you have terrible hand writing. I can hardly read this. Just like your dad."

"He says the same thing," Rhiannon said. "But he blames your side of the family."

Starla laughed. "Come on. You can't be late for school. How do you feel this morning? Still sore from the bucking machine?"

"A little bit. I don't know why Janet is so set on being Ms. Rodeo Queen. Maybe she's more in shape than me."

"She's been doing this since she was a child. She's probably just used to it."

"Could be why she's so nasty all the time. Her muscles hurt!"

"Rhiannon Selene." Starla hesitated then laughed. "You might be right."

CHAPTER TWENTY SIX

"My brain is just, well, full," Rhee said in greeting to her friends. "Don't expect witty conversation, because I got nothing." They had ten minutes before the bell rang for school to start. "I don't know how I'm going to retain anything the teachers say today."

"What? We're supposed to remember that crap?" Corey grinned.

"Why?" Melody asked, ignoring Corey. She dropped her back pack at her feet.

"I had this crazy dream."

"Me, too," Bonnie said. "I was tall, and had perfect eyesight. I didn't want to wake up."

Rhiannon laughed. "You have contacts. Why haven't you been wearing them?"

"Pure laziness. Being pretty requires a lot of work." She leaned closer, even though Corey wandered off to talk to some guys by the stairs. "Beautiful, I mean. I've been doing the spell and I swear Corey has been paying more attention to me."

The fact that Bonnie's budding confidence made her more flirtatious and fun was probably the draw, but Rhiannon kept her opinion to herself. "Awesome." They high-fived. "I was a goddess."

"So you don't want this anymore?" Melody pulled a green dream catcher from the backpack and dangled it in front of Bonnie.

"Hey, that's so cool. Did you make it for me?" Bonnie accepted the dream catcher, admiring the details. "Feathers, glass beads, leather, twine and green string." She looked up, her eyes bright. "Thanks!"

Melody blushed, obviously pleased. "Here, Rhee, I have one for you too. Blue and silver." She handed it over, as if shy to give something hand crafted.

The instant Rhiannon touched the webbed hoop, powerful positive mojo filled her. "Whoa. Where did you make these?" It didn't have the darker energy Rhee associated with Mel.

Melody crossed her arms. "I don't even want to know why you asked the question that way. But, as it turns out, I was at my grandma's."

Bonnie and Rhee exchanged a look.

"And?" Rhee prompted, surprised.

"She showed me how to make them. There's even a little incantation you say or think as you are tying the knots." She lifted her shoulder and let it fall as if it wasn't very important, but Rhee got it. Melody, stepping outside her self-imposed boundaries?

"A spell!" Bonnie said excitedly. "Native American Magic, meet Wiccan magick." She pointed from Mel to Rhee.

"Not magic," Melody said quickly. "This is different. This is *tradition*."

Rhee changed the subject. "So why were you there? That's great, I mean, but you've been kind of hanging close to town." In other words, avoiding the Indian Reservation as if it had the plague.

Uncomfortable, Melody shuffled her feet. "Mom made me go. Wanted me to listen to Grandma's advice about Dad."

"That's a good idea," Bonnie said. "Get another opinion."

"I totally didn't want to go, but when she called and asked me, herself, I couldn't say no. And we ended up having the best visit! She showed me how to makes those." Mel jerked her head toward the dream catchers.

"They're awesome. I know Mom will want to carry them in the shop, if you're willing. Handcrafted artisan dream catchers made by the Kiniwick tribe? You could probably get fifteen to twenty bucks a piece."

Melody's defensive stance relaxed. "Ya think?"

Bonnie nodded. "Why not? You have great detail, and the more expensive the materials you use, the higher the price."

"You would be an entrepreneur!" Rhee grinned. "Already a zillionaire by the time you hit college."

"I don't care about that so much," Melody laughed. "But hello, car."

"So," Rhee checked the time on her vintage Swatch. "We have like two minutes before the bell rings. Did Grandma change your mind about seeing your dad?"

"She doesn't judge people, although she understands why I feel the way that I do. She says that Dad has his reasons, too. Which didn't make anything clearer, you know? But she asked me to keep an open mind, and heart." Melody curled her lip as she tapped her chest.

"What did you say?" Bonnie breathed out.

"I'd think about it."

Rhee chuckled. "Why did I know that was coming? You've made a lot of changes, Mel."

"I wasn't crazy about that girl you described at my house the other day. I don't want to see the glass as empty. So I'm filling it up."

The bell clanged, making the girls jump.

"The conversation can be continued later," Melody said. "Or never. See you guys at lunch?"

They raced inside, Rhiannon hurrying to her locker. She tossed in her coat, and hung the dream catcher on a separate hook. Melody created a work of art. Who knew where it could lead?

She shut the locker and turned around, coming nose to nose with Caleb. "Oof!"

"Sorry," he said automatically. He'd been paying attention to a pretty blonde girl, not where he walked. "It's you, Rhiannon," he mumbled, face scarlet with embarrassment.

"Yeah. Just me." Rhee nodded a greeting at the girl, who frowned. *Ah, another one who doesn't like me, courtesy of Janet and the Roberts clan.* Caleb and Jared were best friends, so it didn't come as a surprise that his new love interest would not be a Rhiannon Godfrey fan.

He paused. "Didn't mean it like that." He dipped his head and looked up with a half smile. "How's Melody?"

"Ah!" The cute blonde huffed and took a step back.

Rhee brought her thumbnail to her teeth. "You could call and ask, you know."

"She refuses to answer my calls. I can take a hint."

It was Rhee's turn to be confused. "Oh, well, I'll tell her you said hi." Did he still care about Melody?

Caleb looked at the impatient blonde. "Don't bother," he told Rhee. "I'm moving on." The girl smiled.

"See ya later then." Rhee waved and turned, not understanding why some things were so difficult. Like high school. And she still had two more years to go!

She passed the office where Principal McGavin waited outside the door, making sure there were no stragglers on the way to class.

Smiling when she saw Rhiannon, she called her over. "Rhiannon! I've been meaning to talk to you. Thank you for supporting the school by joining the riding team. I know it probably wasn't easy, but Janet promised to be nice." Her mouth twitched.

"You knew about it?"

"Yes, I was the one who suggested she contact you. Janet has to have so many activities to get her scholarship into college. She's looking at some prestigious universities, so her high school education needs variety."

Janet hadn't mentioned needing anything for herself. Not a big shock, Rhee acknowledged. "Just to qualify, which is tomorrow morning. I may not make the cut."

"You will." Principal McGavin gave an encouraging nod. "I have to ask, though, what prompted you to agree? School spirit? When we talked about you taking a more active part in Crystal Lake High I certainly never imagined this."

Rhiannon sighed as the late bell rang. "Me either. But she said that if we win the championship, four kids get sponsored for summer camp."

Principal McGavin's brow winged upward in surprise. "Really?" She gestured for Rhee to follow her into her office. "I'll write you a note."

"You seem surprised."

"I don't remember seeing that in the paperwork. I'll check and get back to you." She handed the tardy slip across the table. "Are you finding it easier to fit in?"

"I'm finding it easier to be myself," Rhee said, picking up the paper.

"That is much more important. Once you find and accept who you are inside, what happens outside becomes more manageable. Too bad I didn't learn that until my thirties."

The principal's face was unlined, but her gray hair suggested her age to be at least fifty. Rhiannon liked her, even if she was strict. "Thanks," she said, hurrying out of the office to class.

Lunch arrived just in time to stop Rhiannon from starving to death. She picked up her lunch bag from her locker and hurried to the cafeteria.

Bonnie and Corey were already seated, steaming trays of macaroni and cheese before them.

"This is one of the few times I wished I'd ordered hot lunch. That smells delicious."

"And fattening." Bonnie offered Rhee a bite.

Rhee took it, letting the cheese melt in her mouth. She closed her eyes, enjoying every calorie. "Divine."

Melody hurried in, a slice of pizza on her plate. "I didn't want to wait in the mac and cheese line. Did you guys see who Caleb's hanging out with? A cheerleader." She huffed and sat down on the bench.

"Yeah, she's cute. And pretty smart too. Get's all A's in English class," Corey offered.

"Corey!" Bonnie elbowed her boyfriend.

"What?"

"You're supposed to tell Melody that the blonde is dumber than a bag of rocks with bad breath."

Rhiannon started laughing, nudging Mel's arm. "Caleb asked how you were doing earlier," Rhee said.

"He did?" Melody stiffened.

"Yeah. He also said that you stopped taking his phone calls. Doesn't sound like he did the dumping, Mel." Rhee looked at her friend with censure. "You could have just told us you didn't like him anymore."

"I do! I mean, I did. I don't anymore."

"Typical complicated Melody answer." Rhee opened her container of apple slices. "Want one?"

"No thanks," Melody said. "I grabbed a brownie. No way am I trading bites."

"Not fair," Rhee said, dropping the apple to her bag with an exaggerated sigh.

They ate lunch, each person in a rush to tell a funny story about something that happened in class. Rhee shared Principal McGavin's revelation about Janet.

"So she needed you not just to qualify, but to make her college essay look good." Corey hummed something Rhee couldn't decipher.

"Would it have mattered, though? I mean, you still would have done it for the kids, right?" Bonnie speared the last cheesy noodle with her plastic spork.

Rhiannon gave that some thought. "I guess. But if she would have been honest about her real reasons, that would have given me the chance to be nice, without being coerced. I still would've done it."

"Sure," Melody said, tearing off a small corner of her brownie and handing it to Rhee. "I would have loved to tell her where to stick that college essay. And I ain't talking about her nose."

Corey hooted and slapped the table, and the girls all laughed as their trash jumped.

"Oh look! We've interrupted play time. Corey, when will you realize that having a straw up your nose just isn't funny?"

Rhee looked from Janet to Corey and laughed some more. "I think it's pretty funny, actually," she said, coming to Corey's defense. She didn't explain why he had the straw there. It was better for everyone.

"For someone who hates us," Melody observed, "You sure find your way by this table a lot."

Caleb's blonde friend stood behind Janet, and – no. It couldn't be. Rhee blinked her eyes, certain she had to be hallucinating.

CHAPTER TWENTY SEVEN

"Felicity?"

A new haircut and dark framed hipster glasses didn't offer enough of a disguise. "That's me."

"What are you doing here?" Melody asked, pushing her tray to the center of the table. She turned around on the bench, ready to get up, in a hurry, if needed.

Rhee put her hand on her friend's forearm, sending soothing waves of cool blue. Melody visibly relaxed.

"Rude!" the blonde girl said, giving Melody the once over.

"Just asking a question," Bonnie clarified.

"Told you I heard a rumor," Corey mumbled.

"I am coming back to Crystal Lake High." Felicity slowly took off her glasses as if she were in a RayBan commercial, revealing deep brown eyes made up to Maybelline perfection.

"When?" Melody asked, the question short and far from welcoming.

"As soon as possible. Next week, maybe."

Rhiannon found the silver lining in the awful situation and jumped up. "Great!"

"It is?" Melody asked, looking at her as if she'd lost her mind.

"Yeah." Rhee rubbed her sore back. "Felicity can go to the qualifications with you, Janet, and we don't even have to nod to one another in the hallway."

Janet looked alarmed. "Not so fast, Rhiannon. You promised that you would help. We are counting on you. No backing out now."

Felicity looked bored. "I told you, Janet, to put my name on the roster."

"You knew about Felicity coming back?" Rhee crossed her arms.

"That it was a possibility. I tried to call you. You didn't return my calls."

Rhee fumed, thinking of all the time she'd spent on the bucking machine when she could have been concentrating on dream demons instead. "When I asked you about it, you said it was nothing."

"Because even if Felicity does come back, it wouldn't be in time to get the team on the list."

"Scheming," Mel said. "You are always scheming."

"Melody, I wasn't talking to you," Janet said with a flip of her ponytail.

"She can offer her opinion," Rhiannon said quickly. "I happen to agree with her, actually."

Janet bit her tongue.

"Janet! Hi Janet!" Two freshmen in matching flannel shirts tied around their waists bounded across the cafeteria. "Hi."

Felicity lifted her lip and said in a snarky tone, "Cute. Like puppies. Were we ever that ridiculous?"

The two girls stopped bouncing and Janet gave her friend a warning look as she put her arms around each of them for a hug. "Felicity, these are the two girls trying out for the riding team. Miranda and Shelby, meet Felicity."

Janet turned the girls toward Rhee and swallowed with a very fake smile. "And this is Rhiannon. She's going to be at the qualifications with us tomorrow. She has the electric bull I was telling you about."

Miranda, slightly taller than Shelby, stepped forward, practically vibrating with energy and enthusiasm.

"Hi, I'm Miranda, my friends call my Mandy, but whatever you want is fine. I loved Psychic Kids, and the episode you were on is my very, very favorite."

"Yeah, I like it too. Scary, though," Shelby said, looking from Janet to Rhiannon, uncertain.

"It was certainly an eye opening episode," Felicity said coldly.

Rhiannon glanced at the girl who had worked behind the scenes with the producer to stir up bad ghosts. Felicity had gotten expelled from school. Why was she so certain she could come back?

Breaking the awkward silence, Rhee spoke to the younger girls. "If we do qualify, then you guys will be able to practice with Janet on the bull, once you have your parent's permission."

Rhiannon was kind of looking forward to seeing Janet on the bull. At very high speed.

"We will, we will," Miranda said with a big smile. "Janet said you are really good."

"She did?" Rhee felt Janet's glare and kept her gaze on the girls. "Well, not as good as Janet. But you two can learn!"

Janet had guts, Rhee would give credit where it was due. She acted as if she and Rhiannon great friends, not mortal enemies, as she herded her group away from the table. "Bye, Rhee. See you in the morning. Do you need me to pick you up?"

Knowing it was killing Janet to act nice, Rhee pretended to consider the option before finally shaking her head. "No, thanks anyway. I've got a ride. Nice to meet you Miranda, Shelby."

As soon as the group left the cafeteria, Rhiannon burst out laughing. "I thought Janet was going to explode."

"Why was she pretending to be nice?" Corey asked, confused.

"Because," Bonnie explained between giggles, "she had to convince those girls that bronco riding was fun, and that it would be a great extracurricular activity. I'm thinking she used Rhiannon as a carrot to get the girls to join."

Corey grinned a doofus grin. "Janet had to use Rhee to be the cool one. Now that is justice."

Melody shook her head. "I don't trust Janet, and I especially don't trust her when she's with Felicity. Can we sign a petition telling Principal McGavin we don't want her back?"

"I don't think so," Rhee said, wishing it was different. "But bullying is pretty serious, and she was manipulating a lot of kids to get her way. I really hope she doesn't show up tomorrow morning."

"Should we come and support you?" Bonnie asked, gathering the trash on her empty tray.

"Please don't," Rhee groaned. "It's embarrassing enough that Dane will be there. Sweat and mud are not attractive."

"I don't know," Corey said with a brow waggle. "I've seen women's wrestling."

Bonnie tossed a wadded up napkin at him. "You are so ridiculous."

"What? Pure entertainment. My heart belongs to you." He kissed her fingers.

"Disgustingly sweet," Melody declared. "I can't come see you anyway, since I'm working with your mom in the house. Something about the shop needing to be fixed?"

Rhee nodded. "Yeah." Her friends were supportive, but preferred quiet, ghostless activities. "Bonnie and Corey, we'll see how I feel after tomorrow's certain humiliation. Maybe we can all get together for a celebration lunch after – if I'm not in a body cast."

"You will be great," Bonnie said proudly. "Hey, how are those statues?"

"I still don't know what's up with them. I'm doing a lot of research." All true, without the details of flying kittens and stacked candles.

"I talked to my grandma about spirits, and about whether or not they could actually live in those statues."

"You did?" Rhiannon leaned forward. Melody, committed to changing, didn't hold back.

"She said that Spirit can inhabit anything. Rocks, trees, a pencil." Melody shrugged. "Anything. And if someone, for example, a shaman in the Native American tradition, invoked the Great Spirit for aid in trapping the bad spirit to a certain object in order to contain it, then it might stay there until the spell is broken."

"You and Rhee aren't that different," Bonnie declared, making the point again.

"We believe in a higher power, we go to church and pray. We chant and sing for certain things to happen," Corey said, slinging his arm around Bonnie's shoulders. "I think we're all pretty similar in here." He lightly pounded his fist against his chest.

"I agree." Rhee bowed her head. "In fact, Wicca, Native American beliefs, Christianity, and Greek mythology are all colliding together over these statues."

"You just had to toss in Ancient Greece." Melody clicked her tongue against her teeth as if Rhee had finally crossed the line.

"Wait until I figure it all out, and then your mind will really be blown." Rhiannon sighed. "Anyway, Mel, make sure you talk to Mom about the dream catchers tomorrow. It would be awesome if you could save for a car."

"Already on my list, Rhee. Oh, Grandma told me something else yesterday that I'm not sure I believe. She said Dad was tormented by demons as a kid, and he uses alcohol to keep them at bay. Instead, that lowers his resistance, so he is pestered by them all the time."

"Demons?" Rhee asked. "Wow."

"I guess he had nightmares. Swore he saw ghosts."

"No way." Rhiannon sat back and looked closely at her friend. "Some people choose not to deal with their paranormal abilities and it makes them sick. Mentally and physically."

"I know what you are thinking, Rhee. Knock it off." Melody shoved her chin out in a stubborn motion. "I am not my father."

CHAPTER TWENTY EIGHT

Rhiannon showed off her new dream catcher as soon as she got home.

"That is beautiful," Starla said. "I hope Melody wants to make a few, and we can see how they do on the on line store, too."

"Thanks, Mom." Rhee gave her mother a one-armed hug before pointing to her dad. "Guess what I found out today?"

Her dad threw his arms to the side. "Hmm. How to spell, or add, or find Antarctica on the map?"

"Funny." Rhee set the dream catcher on the table by the couch. "No. None of those typical school things. I found out that Janet totally faked her reasons for needing me on the team. She's actually applying to big universities and needs to show a commitment to an activity she excels at."

Her parents laughed, and her mom said, "Thank the Goddess! I worried about her motivation."

"And it was Principal McGavin who suggested Janet coerce me into being on the team. But the best part was meeting the two freshman today – oh, wait, Felicity was at school today!"

Her mom's bracelets went wild as Starla clasped Rhee's hands and shook them. "No."

"I'm surprised she was allowed. To visit?" Miles asked, seeking for reasons.

"She said she's coming back." Rhee disentangled herself from her mom and tossed her hands upward. "Monday, maybe."

"She was supposed to spend the rest of the year at that private school for kids in trouble." Starla's mouth thinned. "I don't blame her entirely for what happened, I think it was that camera man, but she is still a wayward soul in need of guidance."

"She's spiteful and mean, and has some psychic ability that she used to deliberately hurt people. A wayward soul, Mom? You've got to be kidding me."

She and her dad exchanged a commiserating glance. Starla tended to look at the bright side.

Of anything.

"I wonder if she should see Dr. Richards. He did so much for you, and still does."

"Mom! That would be inviting a viper into the bird nest. Sheer destruction. I don't want her at the institute."

"You have such a way with words, honey," her mom said with a smile. "Oh, I talked to Dr. Richards about the connection between Morpheus and Selene. He seemed excited that you'd put them together. Said it made sense, but then had to go. Talking to that man on the phone is next to impossible. He's always got somebody waiting."

"He's busy. He's good at what he does." Rhiannon was so grateful that her parents had found him for her when she'd been a kid of six. "I have to practice that stupid machine, Dad, then shower before Dane gets here. Hey, did I tell you that a symbol of the Moon Goddess Selene is the bull?" She shook her head, hopping back on tangent. "I reminded the girls, they seem so young," Rhee sighed, "that they will have to get permission before they can train with Janet."

"Good." Miles studied the dream catcher, and the shape of the web. "This is very intricate. Each knot, each string cross-sectioned with another. I have some questions for Melody tomorrow."

"She said there's a spell in each one to trap a spirit trying to enter your head while you sleep."

"And yet she won't touch magick." Starla gave a sad shake of her head.

"Don't give up on her Mom! I think she might come around."

At six p.m. on the dot, the truck horn blared from outside, alerting the Godfrey's that Dane had arrived.

Freshly showered with a dusting of eye shadow and powder, Rhiannon ran out the front door and down the steps, throwing her arms around Dane in an exuberant hug the second he jumped down from the cab of the truck. "You're here, you're here!"

His dad honked the horn again, waving, but not able to stay and visit. His schedule as a truck driver was tight. Deliveries waited for no man.

"Dad says he would love to take you all out to lunch on Sunday, as a thank you for having me."

"That sounds great," Rhiannon said. "But not necessary. I should buy him stock in McDonald's for driving you here and dropping you off."

"McDonalds?" Dane laughed, capturing her lips in a kiss. "Dad does not need any more fast food. I'm trying to get him to eat healthy. I even packed him turkey sandwiches for the road."

"That's better, sure. I just know how he likes his double cheeseburgers."

"Four of them at a time got to be too much. I don't care if they are on the dollar menu. He's my only family, and I want him to stick around."

They walked inside the house, shoulder to shoulder, their slow strides in tandem. Rhee appreciated her folks waiting in the kitchen to give her and Dane time alone.

"Are you ready for tomorrow?"

"As ready as I can be. I'm at my time for last year, which means that I will barely squeak by."

"It'll be nice for Janet to owe you one." He kissed her again. "Or ten."

Warm from the toes up, Rhee loved being in the circle of Dane's arms. He made her feel cherished. Special. Like it was completely okay for her to be Rhiannon Selene Godfrey – no matter what that looked like.

Scientist, teenager, witch. "Dream divination."

"Excuse me? Did I miss a thought process?"

"Woops." Rhee giggled. "I'm adding a new skill to my bag of tricks."

"Dream divination? I thought you weren't interested in that?"

"Yeah. Totally not. But the statues have taken over Mom's shop. I'm trying to figure out what to do with them through dreams, since that is the Oneiroi's mode of communication. But last night, instead of Morpheus, I got Selene."

"The Moon Goddess?"

He sank down to the front porch step, pulling her beside him, and hugging her close to keep away the chill. Fifty was cold.

"Yeah. I was her, she was me. It was cool, but I didn't get any big revelation. Lots of temples. Maybe that's the connection?"

"Want me to help you kick some dream demon butt?"

"Well, yes. What do you think I've waiting for?" Rhiannon laughed, clasping Dane's hands between hers. His fingers, long and pale, intertwined with hers.

"I will help, it's what I do."

"Thanks. Seriously, I feel like I'm on the cusp of understanding what to do. It just has to come together, you know? I can't force it, or make it happen sooner. But if it doesn't happen soon, I feel like something bad will happen."

"Like what?"

Rhiannon shrugged, feeling silly. "If I knew, then I'd have another clue to the freaking mystery. Wanna go see the statues?"

"I thought you'd never ask."

"We should tell Mom." Rhee sighed. "But she will have reasons why we shouldn't go."

"Let's just mention it, and see what your parents say. Who knows, they might be curious too."

As it turned out, they were. After the hugs and welcomes for Dane, Rhee suggested a tour of Celestial Beginnings.

Her mom was surprisingly willing. "I wanted to see how things are, but waited, just in case. Your dad told me about the stacked candles and flying quilts."

"I've peered in the windows, but I can't see anything. Makes me wonder if they covered them from the inside."

"Clever." Rhee looked at her dad and nodded. "Well, then, let's do it."

Thor meowed, proclaiming his disapproval.

Hand in hand, Rhiannon and Dane led the way out the back door toward the shop. Her mom and dad stayed close behind. She stopped at the door, and twisted the knob.

"Still locked," Rhee said, mentally unlocking it. At the loud click, she turned the handle again.

Surprised flurries of noise and movement greeted her immediate flicking on of all the lights.

Caught unaware, the stuffed winged kittens flew at their heads with half hearted energy, falling short of the mark.

The strong, warring scents of oils and candles permeated the room while the quilts sailed over the counter and baskets tumbled in a colorful array of fabric.

"Oh," Starla muttered. "I warned them not to ruin anything!" She kept hold of Miles as she glared around the room.

"Did you stack the books like that?" Dane asked, pointing to the tower that went all the way up to the ceiling of the barn.

"I snuck over here in my spare time," Rhee teased. "I liked playing with blocks as a kid."

"It seems wobbly." Dane stepped back to take in the room. "Definitely occupied by something other than us. What do they want?"

The books dropped to the ground with a thunk, one by one.

"Be nice to the books," Starla said with a click of her tongue.

The books continued to fall until a separate energy gathered them to put on the shelves.

"Good, or bad, or indifferent?"

"If I knew, Dane, then I could make progress." She eyed the couch, which was missing some cushions.

"It doesn't feel malevolent. Just," Dane looked around, "Messy."

A fiery brush of air raced past them, hurtling cushions and books toward them. Surprised by the force of anger, the four of them ran for the door, filing out in haste before turning around to see if the demons followed them.

The door slammed shut.

"Okay. That last one? Could be a jerk."

Rhee, nerves on high alert, nodded. "Kind of how I feel about it too." She slipped her hand in Dane's. "This is why I can't get a good read on what they want from me. It's like the three of them don't know, either."

"Chaotic energy. Maybe being trapped in those statues for so long has made them crazy?"

"Just what we need," Rhee said. "Lunatic dream demons."

Starla clapped her hands together and started walking back to the house. "It's a good thing we closed the shop for tomorrow. Now, who is ready for dinner?"

Thor followed behind them, meowing in his deep throaty way. "I guess he is, Mom."

Tension settled over them as they filed into the kitchen. "I didn't understand what you were talking about, Rhee," Dane said. "Now I do. We have to come up with a plan."

"You think?" Rhee let a little bit of sarcasm through in her tone. She propped her chin in her hand. "We've been trying all week. Answers are not that forth coming."

"Dream journaling is great," Dane said, tapping her notebook of last night's dream. "That's how Dennis talked to me."

"Sleep is when we are most vulnerable." Rhee shivered. "I don't want to leave my psyche open for attack."

"That's why you need help." Dane pointed to his chest. "And now I'm here. I reflect what you feel, your power." He grabbed the pen and paper. "Let's do this."

CHAPTER TWENTY NINE

Dinner, television, making out in the barn while bedding down the animals, made the time fly by. "It's midnight." Rhee forced herself to go to her room. They'd made it as far as the bottom of the stairs. "Good night, Dane."

"Night Rhee."

His arms around her waist, her arms looped around his neck, their mouths warm and familiar. They kissed again.

"I have to go to bed," Rhee whispered, leaning her forehead against his. "I'm literally dreaming for an answer to the problem. If you hear any screaming, wake me up, would you?"

"Fine." He broke away, ever the gentleman. "But for the record, I would rather make out some more."

"So noted." Rhee's belly tumbled with emotions she didn't have time to sort through. But man, did she like Dane.

He pushed her up the stairs to her room, and he went to the couch. "Don't forget to set your alarm. Eight good?"

"I'll do it for seven thirty, just in case."

She waved her fingers at him and got ready for bed. The journal sat beside her bed. Waiting.

What would she dream about? Selene, again?

Would Morpheus break through, and appear before her to show his side of the story?

Rhee lay back, punched her pillow into submission, and closed her eyes.

She counted sheep.

She counted winged demon statues.

Opening her eyes, she looked at the clock. One a.m.. This was not good. Rhiannon always slept well.

Her feet tingled, then her nose itched.

At last she got up and decided to read by moonlight, hoping to tire her racing mind. The moon goddess book was still on the windowsill, so Rhee picked it up, thumbing through the pages to find where she'd left off.

"Mount Latmia," she told Thor, who didn't look like he much cared.

They were *supposed* to be in bed.

She read a few pages, chuckling softly. "Ah yes, the gorgeous mortal Selene loved. Endymion. She had a lot of lovers, it seemed, but I guess that might happen over a couple thousand years."

Rhiannon wondered as she read if Morpheus, a very handsome god, and Selene, a renowned beauty, had ever hooked up. Might explain a different connection.

"Ancient gods and goddesses."

She read further, and didn't notice when the book fell from her relaxed fingertips.

Dream, Rhiannon, dream.

Selene's bright figure, with the crescent moon on top of her head like bull horns, dismounted from the silver chariot. Her winged horses stilled, their majestic heads bowed as plumes of white breathed out their nostrils.

Manes of shining bright silken strands, so fine as to be incandescent spider's webs, danced in a slight breeze.

Rhiannon reached out to touch them, her hand sliding through the image with no substance. Disappointed, Rhee realized she was separate from Selene, yet still in a position to watch. Observe.

They'd arrived outside the temple of the Oneiroi. Selene strode across the raked white stone in thin soled leather sandals criss-crossed up her calves. Her tunic came to the knee, and attached over one shoulder, leaving the opposite arm bare. Rhiannon followed as the goddess entered the temple, her temper clear in each strong foot fall shaking the foundation.

"Where is Morpheus?" Selene called to a cowering acolyte.

"Sleeping," he said.

"Sleeping? His duty is to guide dreams, and when does one do that? While mortals sleep. It is night, servant. Morpheus needs be awake, and to me, within moments, or I will tear this temple down!"

Rhiannon responded to Selene's display of temper by leaning forward in recognition. Sometimes it felt good to just yell.

And if you were a goddess, nobody told you to control yourself.

The boy servant returned, being dragged by a furious winged figure. "You dare, Selene?"

"I do, Phobetor." Selene jutted her chin. "I know you and your lunatic brothers tried to capture my horses. Who else but the creator of nightmares would upset my household with stories of demons? I demand to speak with Morpheus for retribution."

"He is not here."

"I thought he slept?"

"A story by an ignorant slave."

"I want justice! Two of my household have jumped from the roof with crazed stories, bedeviled, and why? I won't sell you my horses."

"We don't want your horses, with wings of our own, we have no need of such transport."

"Then why try to steal them? They are important to me! I bring the moonlight across the night sky."

Phobetor spread his wings and arms out to the side and smiled a secretive smile. "Perhaps a spurned lover?"

Selene's own wings bristled and puffed with anger. "I love Endymion, as you know."

"Right. We granted him the gift of sleep so he can stay eternally young. And what did you do for us?"

"Zeus spoke to Hypnos, who ordered you to see it done. My gratitude is to Hypnos. You and your brothers are lackeys." Selene's wings extended far beyond the width of Phobetor's.

Yet his fury outmatched that of the Moon Goddess. "Your lover doesn't dream of you," he spat. "But of monsters and goblins, and death."

Frightened, Rhiannon wished she could pull the goddess backward, and out of the Oneiroi temple. From the corner of her eye she saw a short winged demon rubbing his hands together as a net of something dark and shadowy drew down from the ceiling, hovering over Selene's head.

"Moon witch. Die, now!" Phantasos yelled.

"Watch out!" Rhiannon called, fear unlike any nightmare she'd ever had rising like bile from her stomach.

Morpheus strode inside the temple, his human features exquisite, his golden hair and wings truly godlike. He stopped the chaos, freezing time with a swing of the Dream Wand. "Brothers, what you have done? Selene, I apologize,"

His words were cut off as Phantasos leapt atop a two headed black dog, riding toward his brother. He stole the staff, using it to cut the hovering shadowy mass hanging above Selene free. It layered like sticky tar over the moon goddess, dampening her silver shine.

But the points of her crescent moon tore free from the trap and she shook her entire body like a wet, furious hound. Her eyes gleamed silver, her gaze diamond hard as she brought her hands together. With thunderous words, she pointed at Morpheus, then Phobetor, and finally Phantasos, turning them into statues and binding their power for eternity.

Thor's low howls woke her from the deep sleep. Her dream journal fluttered back and forth on the end table, her pen rolling across the floor to land at her feet. Slumped in the chair, she straightened and assessed the situation.

Her own psychic energies made the journal move, triggered by fear and helpless anger. As she calmed, thinking of blue and white and chamomile tea, the energy in the room calmed too.

Thor brought her the pen, holding it gently in his mouth as he leaped to the ledge. She held out her hand, calling for her journal.

She looked up at Thor and shook her head. "I think Selene is the one who bound the Oneiroi to the statues."

Rhee frowned, wondering where the statues themselves had gone. "We are going to have to search Celestial Beginnings from top to bottom. I can't force them back if I can't find them."

Thor's tail swished, slowly, encouragingly.

"Which isn't the least of my problems." She looked at the clock, which blinked six a.m.. "Once I find them, how do I capture their spiritual entity and force them back?"

Rhee narrowed her eyes.

"And why won't Morpheus speak to me? Am I too far away?"

She shivered. "The last place I want to sleep is in the shop while it's being..." Exhaling, she accepted her fate. "Haunted by those missing dream demons." Remembering the scrapes and bites from the stuffed kittens, Rhee shuddered. How to protect herself?

The dream catcher she'd hung from the light pull by her closet until she could find a better place swung as if touched by a light wind.

Thor's tail flicked straight upward.

Rhiannon grinned and scratched his ears. "It's a plan."

CHAPTER THIRTY

Rhiannon dotted extra powder beneath her eyes to camouflage the circles from lack of sleep. Dressed in a black and silver plaid flannel shirt, jeans, red cowboy boots and a red tee shirt, she felt dressed for the part.

Hair in two braids, with a side sweep of bangs, a swish of gloss for her lips and down the stairs she went.

Her mom, dad and Dane were all up and sitting around the kitchen table.

Dane looked adorable in a black tee and jeans, his dark hair hitting his shoulders. He smiled, his gray eyes framed by ink black lashes, his skin pale. "Morning."

"You make me look tan," Rhee said, blowing him a kiss from the threshold.

"I heard you pacing." Starla turned, mixing bowl in hand. "I hope you got some sleep."

"Did you dream anything journal worthy?" Dane buttered a slice of toast, then added strawberry jam. "I dream about this jam, Starla."

Her parents insisted Dane call them by their names, something her other friends hadn't gotten comfortable with yet.

"Homemade tastes better," her mom said with an appreciative smile. "And it's better for you. We grew those strawberries."

Rhee answered Dane's question, eyeing his toast. "As a matter of fact, I have an idea on how to catch the loose Oneiroi."

"Yippee!" Starla finished whisking eggs and milk. "How, when?"

"Tonight. I want to have a supernatural sleepover."

Her dad choked on his coffee. "What?"

Dane's smile widened. "Sounds good."

"I'm not sure." Her mom glanced at the kitchen clock. "We need to get you fed, first."

"I can't eat much," Rhee said, rubbing her belly. "After would be better. I need a dozen or so dream catchers, made with poppy oil to attract the Oneiroi."

"I don't understand," Miles said slowly.

"Dream catchers are spirit catchers," Dane jumped in with the right answer and Rhee nodded.

"Bingo. We can hammer out the details after I get home, but Mom, if all goes well, we can have the statues bubble wrapped and on their way to Athens tomorrow."

"You want to send them back to Greece?" Miles lifted his brow, not certain if she was serious.

"I don't know." Rhee snagged the perfect bite of toast from Dane's fingers, quickly putting it in her mouth to chew. "Mm. Strawberry bliss, Mom."

"Thief." Dane took another piece of toast from the stack and shook it at her before starting the butter and jam process all over again.

"How do you feel, Rhiannon?" Her dad took another drink of coffee. "Ready to take on the bronco?"

"Uh, no. But I can qualify us and then get Janet out of my hair. Principal McGavin will be happy, and then I can forget about it."

"One thing at a time. Should I ask Melody about the dream catchers?" Her mom poured the egg mixture into a hot skillet.

"I'll text her from the car, but you will probably have to explain a little better. And take her to buy materials? I'll help make them if she can show me how. I can tie a knot."

"Me too! Knot spells are easy for something quick." Stirring the eggs, her mom hummed beneath her breath.

"Good to know," Dane said, shielding his toast from Rhee's prying fingers. At her look, he relented and gave her half.

"Thank you. I can't tell if I'm hungry or nervous. If I eat your toast, then I don't have to commit until I'm sure."

Dane laughed while Miles lowered his iPad where he read the news. "Rhiannon, that takes commitment issues to a new level."

"Here. This should tempt you." Her mom slid a small plate of perfect, fluffy scrambled eggs dusted with cheese in front of her nose.

Rhee's stomach gave a definitive rumble. "Yup. I'm hungry."

"Not too much, with all of that jerking around. I'll make a big lunch."

"Good idea! Corey and Bonnie can come over. We'll draft them into making dream catchers with us."

She'd just finished her eggs when her phone rang. "Janet," she predicted, answering the phone with dread. "Hello?"

"Are you coming?"

"Yes. I just finished breakfast."

"I don't know how you could eat without throwing up. Explains why you are so much bigger than me."

Rhee rolled her eyes. "Why are you calling me?"

"The girls are asking where you are."

"I have a half an hour."

"Just come."

Rhee stared at her phone. "She hung up on me." Standing, Rhiannon took her plate to the sink. "I've been summoned."

Starla laughed and kissed her cheek. "You will be amazing. I put a little nutmeg for good luck in the eggs."

"They tasted great. I hope they work."

Miles drove the five minutes to the fairgrounds where school busses of kids were parked.

Dane whistled low. "Wow. I didn't know bronco riding was even legal, and here it is a country sport."

Miles lifted his video camera. "I'm ready."

"Dad, if I fall off too soon, you have to delete that film. Or if I look gross. Trash it."

He pretended not to hear her and said in an exaggerated drawl, "Go get 'em cowgirl." Then he pointed to the fenced in area. "I'll be in the stands setting up. I have to get the lighting right."

"Thanks Dad."

"I'll be right there." Dane turned to Rhiannon and gave her a good luck kiss. "Don't hurt anything." He heard a scraping sound as one of the high strung horses attempted to break free of the stall, hooves splintering wood. "They look mad."

"What took you so long?" Janet, followed by Miranda and Shelby, came from the closest barn. She noticed Dane and pretended to smile. The younger girls grinned and blushed.

Dane said hello, wished Rhee luck once more, and wandered over to the bleachers.

"He is so cute," Miranda said.

"Yeah," Shelby seconded.

"Excuse me girls," Janet snapped her fingers. "Let's think horses, not boys. Now, we have our own team table by the judges, so pay attention to how the other girls do, okay?" Janet looked at Rhee. "You just have to sign; I filled out the rest of the paperwork for you."

Rhiannon realized how important this event was to Janet, enough for her to ask for Rhiannon's help despite the hostility between them. "Thanks. Last night I hit last year's time, so I'm feeling better. The first few days on the bull I thought I was going to die."

Miranda's eyes widened.

"She's exaggerating," Janet said quickly.

"It's actually super fun," Rhee amended. "You wear a helmet and pads and it feels like you're flying."

Grateful, Janet nodded and led them to the table. Felicity sat behind them, not officially a part of the team.

Rhiannon watched the horses come in, and out, and the girls hang on as long as they could before getting tossed. Rodeo clowns popped in and out of colored barrels.

"That team there is really good," Janet said, her green gaze intense. "They still have a senior and a junior, but ours graduated last year, and Sarah, a junior, broke her leg." She swallowed and shaded her eyes. "Thanks."

Rhee figured that was the best she'd get and nodded. She'd only learned how to do this sport out of spite – to prove to Janet a city girl could handle the pressure. It seemed karmic that they'd work together now. "Sure."

"For Crystal Lake High School, Rhiannon Godfrey!" Rhee tightened her helmet, smoothed her gloves and with the aid of a few trained cowhands, got on her horse.

Her stomach was solid as a drum, her grip on the reins tight. Mouth dry and eyes closed, Rhiannon felt the jolt of her horse as the starter gun went off and the stall door opened.

Dirt, horse sweat, leather, hay. Forcing herself to keep her eyes open instead of tightly closed, Rhiannon accepted her fear, then used it to become one with the horse's movements.

She wasn't great, but she was good enough, lasting the ten seconds needed to qualify, plus two. She felt her gloves slipping on the slim leather reins and leaped to the side, out of the path of the horse's hooves. Jumping up from her roll in the dirt, she glanced around and waved at her dad and Dane, who cheered like she'd won a blue ribbon.

Running back to the team's table, where Janet and the girls gave her high fives, Rhiannon took her seat.

Felicity's bad vibes crossed across the air with ease, but then Principal McGavin joined them.

"Well done, Rhiannon. Janet, when will you go?"

"In a few minutes, as champion, I go last." Janet answered without any extra attitude, just fact, and the younger girls looked at her with admiration.

Rhiannon pointed to Felicity. "Will it be any problem to have Felicity added when I quit?"

"You can't quit!" Miranda tugged on Rhee's arm.

Principal McGavin frowned. "Felicity is not coming back until next year." She looked from scowling Felicity to a red faced Janet. "I thought I was clear on that yesterday in my office."

Janet swallowed. "You were."

Rhee crossed her arms, her hip throbbing from her fall. She bruised easy, so no doubt it would blossom into a painful purple flower. Bronco riding was not something she did for fun. "Janet," she said.

"Can we talk later, please? I can't be upset before I ride." She flipped her hair, which was held back in a long blonde pony tail.

"Of course," Principal McGavin said. "I was just stopping by to congratulate you. I know how hard you worked putting this together."

"Thanks." Janet smiled but it didn't reach her eyes.

The principal left and Janet held up her hand, effectively blocking Rhiannon's questions. "I don't want to talk about it."

"That works for you?" Rhiannon tilted her head, but applauded with Janet's name was called. She and the other two girls watched as she executed flawless technique before gaining twenty seconds.

"She's so good," Shelby breathed out.

"We are totally going to win," Miranda said. "I can't wait to start practice." She looked at Rhee. "Can you?"

Rhee didn't want to lie, but there was no freaking way she was going to let Janet trick her into staying on the team.

"It will be a lot of fun," Rhee said, choosing her words carefully.

She heard a rumble of male laughter and looked to her left. Jared, in his element in boots and cowboy hat, tipped his hat. "Score one for the Roberts."

CHAPTER THIRTY ONE

"I can't believe it. The paperwork I signed without reading the fine print says there is no changing of the roster. Sarah's name is on it, so if she miraculously heals in super human time, she can finish out the year. I am *stuck*."

What stung worse than anything was the look of satisfaction on Jared's face.

Dane put his arm around her shoulders. "You did good! Think of the kids."

"If you really want out, I can talk to the principal tomorrow."

"Dad, I can fake an injury, which would be better than denying Principal McGavin her school spirit."

"Bad karma." Her dad unlocked the doors to his black BMW. "Want to risk it?"

"I am too busy to be injured, anyway." Rhiannon took the back seat, letting Dane have shotgun.

She pouted for the five minutes going home, but pulled herself together as soon as they arrived at the house. Her mom met them at the door.

"Well?" Starla hugged Rhee close. "How did it go?"

"Yeah, how was it?" Melody asked, a pair of scissors in her hand.

Rhee took a deep breath, then released all the negative energy. "Janet is a jerk." Inhale, exhale. "But I made the time to qualify." Inhale, exhale. "You can come see me when we have our first competition in two weeks."

"But I thought," Starla interrupted then quieted. "Oh no. She tricked you?"

Melody tossed her head back and laughed. "We knew it, we knew she was up to something. And you can't get out of it?"

"I'm sure I could find a way – but, as you know, I need to concentrate on something else right now. Did Mom explain?"

Melody pointed to the stack of willow hoops in varying sizes. "Enough for two dozen. Assorted string, beads and Grandma said we could call her when it was time to do the incantation. She Skypes." Mel shrugged. "With a cousin in Montana. I had no idea. I mean, during the summer she lives in a freaking teepee."

Dane grinned. "She sounds awesome. Are you giving us a tutorial on how to do this so we can help?"

"You got it." Melody pointed to the supplies in the living room. "We've spread everything out."

"And you aren't wigged out by the shop, and the spirits?"

"You know it isn't my favorite, but I'm not going to stick my head in the sand and ignore what's happening. You've made that pretty much impossible since you moved here." Melody put her hand on her hip. "Congratulations on making the team, by the way."

"You are not funny," Rhiannon decided. "I'm showering."

She heard her dad say, "Wait until you see what I captured on video."

Dane said, "We are talking YouTube gold."

Rhee groaned.

The shower restored her good mood. She dressed comfortably, but still cute, in jeans and a fitted Henley. She didn't bother with shoes, letting her toes stretch in comfy socks. The bruise on her hip hurt, and was turning a bright raspberry color.

All in all, she counted the ride as a success, and pushed the rest from her mind.

Skipping makeup made her look twelve so she swiped some brown liner and black brown mascara on. "Good enough," she told herself. She went downstairs, her hair still damp, but brushed back from her face.

Dane and Melody were head to head, his black hair and her dark brown almost touching as she showed him how to start the leather strip around the willow hoop.

Her mom and dad sat on each end of the couch, with mugs of tea or coffee and a spool of sinew between them. Starla looked up. "Three yards of sinew each," she explained. "Dad and I are cutting."

"We watched a video on YouTube. I think you could figure out how to build a spaceship from the information there." Her dad sounded intrigued, which worried her. "I bet I could find a video on how to fix the barn, next time it leaks."

She and her mom exchanged a quick look of panic, then Rhee laughed it off and walked toward Dane and Mel. "Did anybody talk to Bonnie?"

"Yeah, she and Corey are coming over. I have never heard anyone so excited about doing crafts."

Rhee wrinkled her nose. "And the spirits?"

"I gave her the bare facts," Mel said. "But you know she would support you even if she had to stand in a freezing cold cemetery parking lot while you faced an invisible whirling dervish." Melody tapped her chin in thought. "Oh yeah. We did that already. We're friends, through thick and thin."

Grinning, Rhee picked up a willow hoop. "Thick and thin. Teach me."

"According to legend," Melody said, "though not our tribe's tradition, the Spider Woman wanted to save her people, so she created a lodge that would capture the early morning dew. Somehow, this became a symbol for capturing bad spirits at dawn. There's a hole in the center so that the good dreams or spirits can come through. I don't know if that will help you or not, Rhee."

"I am taking a plunge of faith on this one. I think the moon goddess wants to right a wrong. Before it is too late?"

"Two thousand years have gone by. Why would there be a time limit now?" Dane's question echoed her own sentiments.

"I don't know." Rhee chuckled. "That seems to be my new mantra."

"For a girl who likes to be in control, that must be hard to swallow, huh?"

Rhee gave Melody a sharp glance. "What are you saying?"

"Control issues." Melody bumped her hip into Rhee, who grimaced. "Are you okay? I'm just teasing."

"I have a bruise. You found it." Rhee rubbed the sore area. "I can take a joke as well as the next person."

"Nobody likes being the butt of any joke," Starla said with a laugh. "It just happens sometimes."

Dane cleared his throat and held up his dream catcher. "So. Eight points for the spider's legs?"

"Yup. Then it's just a matter of pulling thread through the hoop. We need to leave some at the end to add the feathers, if you want."

"I want to catch me some ancient Greek gods," Rhee declared. "I'd like the red yarn, for Poppy."

"We bought red feathers, and silk poppy flowers," Starla said, pointing to the piles of decorations. "And the oil."

"Morpheus's symbol is the poppy, so that's good," Rhee said. Before she could start wrapping her willow hoop, the doorbell rang.

"Come in!" She knew it had to be Bonnie and Corey. Instead, there was an insistent knock at the door.

Rhee walked over and opened it, expecting to see her friends with full hands or something. "Janet?"

"I know, I am not your favorite person." She handed over a wrapped box. "You probably cast a spell on me or something, or whatever it is you people do." She tossed her ponytail impatiently. "I just, well, wanted to apologize."

Accepting the gift as if it might contain a poisoned snake, Janet stepped back with a roll of her eyes. "Don't worry. Nothing deadly in there. Like an asp. Or a rattler."

She left, her mom, strained mouth and all, driving. Bonnie and Corey drove past them as they came toward the house.

"We're grand central," Rhee joked, holding the box with an exaggerated concerned look.

Bonnie hopped out of the car before it was barely stopped. "Was that Janet?"

"Yeah."

"I can't believe it," Corey said. "She didn't flip me the bird for the first time since fifth grade."

"She's feeling guilty." Rhee lifted the box.

"Hurry up already!" Dane yelled. "We want to know what's inside. A bomb?"

"Her mom was driving, if I die. Get her for an accomplice to murder." Rhee brought the gift inside. Her parents were stuck on the couch with yards of sinew, Dane and Melody each had their hands busy with dream catchers. She looked at Corey and Bonnie. "Here we go."

She lifted the lid. Inside was a pair of sterling silver crescent moons, courtesy of the Dream Boutique in downtown Tilton. "These are really nice. What does it mean if I keep them?"

"You're going steady," Dane teased.

"How thoughtful!" Starla said, her head tilted to the side.

"I already have a boyfriend," Rhee reminded everyone. "But these are really cool."

"I am so glad I was here to see this. I never, in a million years, despite all the spooky mooky stuff you've put us through, would have believed Janet Roberts could be nice." Bonnie crossed her arms, a look of hope on her face.

"Don't fall for it!" Melody shouted, her cheeks red.

Corey laughed. "Hey Dane. Welcome to the mad house."

"I love it here," Dane said with a wink at Rhee.

"So what are we doing?" Corey asked, shrugging out of his jacket to hang it on the hook, automatically reaching for Bonnie's as if they'd been married a zillion years.

She handed it over with a smile. "Thanks, Cor. Do we choose colors?"

"You can pick how many feathers and how big you make your net. Everything else is the same," Rhee said. "We want to lure the demons in with poppy red and trap them come daylight. I hope to put them into their statues and bind them again, so they can't wander. I'm thinking after two thousand years, they just got loose."

"Do you need us to help you with that?" Bonnie asked bravely.

Rhee put her arm around her friend and squeezed. "Nope. This is just the perfect amount of help."

They worked, hands busy, mouths going. Rhee's mind freely wandered over the giant holes in her plan as she pulled the sinew through the hoop, over and over, creating a magical web inside, with a hole the size of a quarter, for the good guys.

What did she want to accomplish? The answer seemed straightforward. To capture the dream demons loose in Celestial Beginnings.

Then what?

That depended on them. What did they want? Rhiannon had a good idea that Selene, her namesake, had trapped the Oneiroi in those statues because they'd tried to steal the chariot's horses, which was how she created moonlight.

Off limits, dudes, Rhee thought.

But to keep the quasi gods trapped for two thousand years, well, that seemed extreme. Then again, Selene rocked the moon goddess world, and managed to maintain a cult in today's times, whereas Morpheus and the gang had fallen out of favor.

CHAPTER THIRTY TWO

"This is the last one." Rhee bit off the final piece of thread, her fingers blistered from the constant back and forth pulling of sinew. Instead of feathers, she'd used the silk poppy flowers.

The living room looked like a craft shop. Feathers, clothes pins, spools of thread and discarded flower stems. Beads, feathers and broken willow hoops.

"Thank the Goddess," her mom said, eyes glazed and two dream catchers at her feet. "I was going to make dinner, but I think we need to order Chinese. Even if does take forty five minutes."

"Way ahead of you," Miles said, waving the menu to their favorite restaurant in Tilton. "I ordered buckets of fried rice and chicken lo mein for the carnivores in the group. Egg drop soup for everybody."

Rhee blinked away the eye strain and rose, her body aching from the brutal work out earlier. The longer she sat, the stiffer she got. "Thank you, guys. I know this wasn't the best way to spend a Saturday."

Dane held out his hand so Rhee could pull him up from his crossed leg position on the floor. His knees popped. "It's all good. But, after we eat, what then? Do we wait for midnight or something?"

"There's no witching hour, that I know of." Rhee looked at her parents, who shook their heads. "I say we feast, then I pop a few melatonin, and crash on the couch in Celestial Beginnings – after we hang up all these dream catchers."

"How will you know to guide the dreams?" Dane asked. "I'm a receptive, which means that when I am with you, I amp your powers. I should be there too. I can record what's happening in case we need it later."

"This isn't the end?" Bonnie asked, her voice lifting.

"The goal for tonight is to capture the Oneiroi in the dream catchers. Tomorrow, or as soon as I wake up, I can transfer their spirits to their statues. Respectively. If I can find them."

"You haven't found them?" Mel asked in a dry tone.

"No. I've been here." Rhee held up red hands. There had been no time to search for statues. "Besides, I'm hoping they will tell us or at least give us a clue."

Melody exhaled. "It gives me something to do, while you are dreaming."

"You don't have to," Rhee said.

"But I can," Melody gave a single, decisive nod. "I feel sort of responsible, because of the dream catchers. I want to know if they work or not."

"It isn't your fault, if it doesn't work." Rhee quickly assured her.

"If it bombs – totally blaming you," Melody said. "But if it works?" She nodded at tapped her chest. "All me."

Everybody laughed.

They pulled up Skype, where Mel's grandma gave a blessing over the dream catchers, and for everyone involved. Glorianna Skye had intelligent, quick brown eyes. She asked the Great Spirit for protection against demons, and to aid Rhiannon in her quest to capture them using the Kiniwick's tradition.

Rhee bowed her head. "Thank you for the blessing, and the spell of good will. For your granddaughter, Melody. Tonight's work is only half way done, and she's offered to help in the shop."

"I am not surprised that a granddaughter of my lineage be strong enough to see this through." In fact, Grandma looked mildly insulted that anyone think otherwise. "Like her father, Melody has fought demons from birth, which is why I have gifted her with so many dream catchers of her own. As a baby, they were drawn to her lively energy but as she grew older, they scared her."

Melody turned as pale as Dane, which scared Rhiannon so much that she held Melody's arm. "Mel?"

Her friend shook her hand off. "What are you saying, Grandma?"

Dark eyes zeroed in on Mel through the miracle of a laptop camera. "You saw ghosts all the time, and spirits. One day, you stopped laughing at them, screaming instead. So I banished them all, protecting you with blessed dream catchers."

"But, I don't dream," Melody said, arms crossed defensively.

"Little bird, everybody dreams," Grandma said. "Good luck, everyone."

There was a moment of quiet, then Melody said good bye, shutting the lap top with a fierce snap.

"I *don't* dream." Her nostrils flared. Rhiannon stepped forward, feeling for Melody with all her extra senses. Pain and feelings of betrayal swamped her.

Bonnie too came forward, slipping her arm around Mel. "It's okay. I think you might dream, but just don't remember."

"Because of some hocus pocus!" Mel's eyes filled with tears. "They lied to me. My mom, and grandma."

"No," Bonnie jumped in. "They protected you. You saw ghosts, until something scared you, they thought it was fine. Once you didn't like it anymore, they protected you as best they could."

Two tears trickled down Melody's tan cheeks. "Bonnie, I don't like ghosts."

"It's all right, Mel. You know they're there, that's all."

Melody burst into tears, and Rhiannon joined the girls in a three way hug.

"I guess I've always known. I still don't like them," Melody said with a sniff.

"They grow on you," Rhiannon said.

"I can't deny they exist. Not anymore." She breathed in, worry surrounding her aura like pea green poison. "Does this mean I'll be bad, like my dad?"

"No!" Starla joined their circle. "You are your own person, Melody, with your own journey, not meant to repeat the steps your parents took. It is a big world, honey, huge, and you need to take your place in it." She enveloped Mel in a hug. "You are a bright star, Melody."

That was her mother's highest compliment of a soul, and something Starla would never say unless she felt it to be true. Rhee stepped back, needing air. She bumped into Dane, then realized Corey and her dad waited, too.

Emotional crisis were not her thing, but she couldn't be happier for Melody, for finally facing her biggest fear. Her dad, genetically, anyway, had a say in her make up. But when it came down to individual choices, everyone had a voice.

The doorbell rang and they all jumped. Her dad grabbed his wallet, seemingly grateful for something to do, and signed for the food. Corey and Dane helped bring the boxes to the dining room table.

Rarely used, they turned on the lights. The official dining room had a big table with ten seats. Great for parties, but otherwise neglected. However, Rhiannon and her friends, and family, soon had the space warm.

CHAPTER THIRTY THREE

Drowsy, Rhiannon laid back on the couch in the sitting area of Celestial Beginnings. The demons had stopped moving things once she and her accomplices started hanging up the dream catchers.

The occasional stuffed cat would fly by, but Rhee easily swatted it to the ground.

"I will find the statues," Mel promised.

"I'm right here," Dane said, hands poised over the iPad. He could record, type or take pictures. In case the paranormal energy messed with the electronics, he also had a pad of paper and a pen. *Beware, demons, beware.*

Quiet now, Rhee felt the effects of the melatonin and chamomile tea. Her body ached from the real live bronco ride, though her heart rejoiced at Janet's apology. Probably Jared's idea too, she realized with a start.

Keeping her eyes closed, Rhee determined to think about Selene. Morpheus. Her spell to keep them bound to the statues.

Three dream catchers hung directly over her head, with the other twenty placed strategically around the large room.

I am here, Rhiannon thought, lowering her shields bit by bit. It wasn't easy being vulnerable. Her dad guarded the front door.

Her mom, Bonnie and Corey waited with an unhappy Thor at the house around the kitchen. He didn't like these spirits, she could tell. Rhee felt a wave of love for her family, strengthening her resolve to put these unhappy spirits to rest. *Tell me what you want, Morpheus, Phobetor, or Phantasos. I am here, I am your vessel.*

Eyes sealed tight, Rhiannon pushed away the loving energy of her family and friends, making room for Morpheus, if he chose to speak.

Tell me where the statues are.

Time passed, and the dream catchers began to move. Swayed by gentle breezes, though there was no air conditioning or drafts inside the barn.

"Tell me," she whispered sleepily. "Where are you?"

The poppy flower closest to her head somehow came loose from the binding and fell to her forehead. Instead of getting up, she kept still, and opened her mind.

She saw the temple of the Oneiroi, the pyramid shape of worship, the stack of marble stones. "A pyramid," she said softly. "Like your temple, where you safeguarded your treasure."

Rhiannon knew with certainty where the statues were. "The candles," she mumbled.

Morpheus, speak to me.

Witch! Came the loud, reverberating answer to her plea.

Phobetor?

Harsh laughter sounded and Rhiannon remembered clearly the stunted demon she'd seen in the temple. He'd been furious, throwing a temper tantrum. A jealous rage?

Phantasos?

She felt hot wind fly around her but remained still, as if deep in slumber. Open to the evil spirit's assault, she did as trained and assimilated different heat levels in response to her words. Similar to dream divination, just another way to learning symbols and clues to understand the dead. The stunted demon loved Selene. Unrequited love.

"I won!" Phantasos' energy blustered.

"Tell me," she whispered, confused. "Explain how you," she shuddered against the onslaught of negative emotion, "you won."

Demonic laughter resounded through the old barn.

"I won! I WON. She is here. She came for me."

Rhee felt her hair lifted on gusts of energy, dark vibrations echoed around her, shaking the couch like a giant hand.

"You won," Rhee said softly. He wanted to see Selene, so he'd called for Rhiannon?

"Witch! Goddess of the Moon, you concede?"

Rhiannon's body was overtaken by another entity, heat entering from her toes and whooshing upward like a blush. Familiar, silver light.

"I am here! Fool."

Rhiannon felt her body rise, the sprout of wings from her back unfold in a mighty declaration of power.

"Selene," the demon said, awed.

"You wanted me, and here I am."

"You made a fool of me!"

"You are a fool. I had nothing to do with it."

The dream demon spluttered. "Even now, your pride risks all – humble yourself, and maybe I will spare your slave's life."

"Slave? You are an idiot. Her power is more than you or I."

Rhiannon, subtly aware of the exchange, wondered if the moon goddess spoke true.

"I wanted,"

Selene interrupted, her voice unexpectedly kind. "I know what you wanted. What you want."

"Is it too much? Still?"

"I gave my love, my heart, to Endymion. You know this to be true. I have no love for another."

"But you do, take others!"

"You love me, as I love the human. Others don't matter, not with a love such as that. I am sorry, for I know the torment such love can give. Pain, agony." Selene fluttered her wings. "And Gods know, deep joy."

"I would know the joy."

"You don't listen, Phantasos. My heart is not mine to give." Tears fell like silver droplets down Selene's cheeks. Her sorrow was true, her regret immense, but not changeable.

"I hate you, as much as I love you." The squat demon spread his dark wings. "Release me."

Selene folded her wings in, like a protective hug. "It is time. I apologize for keeping you captive for so long."

The room in the air seemed to come together in a sigh. "And my brothers?"

"Them, too."

"The statues?" Her dad asked, having come closer.

"The candle display," Dane said, his eyes never leaving hers.

Melody quickly took down the display, and sure enough, the three statues were hidden inside. Rhiannon hadn't looked there because it hadn't been torn apart like everything else. Lesson learned.

Melody lifted all three and brought them to the couch.

The spirits rushed to the statues, the dream catchers stopping them before they could go any further. A roar of rage exploded above her head as they struggled.

Rhiannon pinched herself, forcing herself awake. "No, they can't stay trapped in the net. They must be freed!"

Caught by the spell in the webs, the Oneiroi thrashed back and forth.

Rhee channeled her namesake, drawing the goddess into her body like a sponge.

Closing her eyes, granting forgiveness and understanding for love unrequited, unresolved, Rhiannon absorbed all negative energy and imagined them all surrounded by an orbit of white, pure love.

Forgiveness, I grant you. Love, I grant you. Freedom, I grant you.

Rhiannon's bright, cleansing energy filled the shop, overtaking anything dark, obliterating the foul intents as well as the deeds.

A hole broke through the roof, allowing the moon's rays to travel directly toward the statues on the couch.

"It is done!" Rhiannon felt Selene overtake her body, felt the oddness of having wings, felt the absolution of moonlight on her flesh as her namesake traveled within the blink of an eye up the star trail to the night sky.

"Bless you, Rhiannon," Morpheus said, his voice resounding around the shop. "We are finally free!"

The statues seemed to gather power, then trembled before they exploded in fragments of ancient marble.

Rhiannon woke up, Dane's arm around her shoulder.

"Are you all right?" His concerned voice reminded her that she was human, his gray eyes reminiscent of her ancient love, Endyriom.

No. *Wait.* "I am Rhiannon Selene Godfrey. Sixteen, female, and,"

Dane kissed her. "Mine."

CHAPTER THIRTY FOUR

"March twentieth, Spring Equinox. A fortuitous time of year," Starla said. "How should we celebrate? I'm filled with energy!"

"I'm tired," Rhee complained. "I don't like being with Janet. My back permanently aches."

Starla patted her belly and Rhee bit her lip. Arguing with her pregnant mom kept getting harder.

How could you win against a baby?

"Listen, Mom, you don't know how demanding it is."

"You are doing a good thing. Building karma. Janet needs you to be amazing so she can get into a great university. So what if she lied to you? I thought we were past this?"

"I practically broke my arm last week!"

"It was a bruise. A bad bruise. And remember how concerned Miranda was? She even sent you a text."

Rhiannon sighed. It had been sweet. "Shelby is the one who actually has talent. And she listens to Janet."

"Who happens to be the champion. Perfect."

"I hate it when you have to be reasonable."

Starla leaned over and gave Rhee's cheek a loud kiss. "I love you."

"I love you, too."

Rhee took a deep breath as she remembered the feel of forgiveness and acceptance by the goddess. "I just don't have to like what you are saying."

Starla nodded, a wise owl smile on her face as she left Rhee and Dane in the living room. "Going for a snack. Pickles. Tuna fish."

They watched her go, then Dane slung his arm around her shoulder. "Spring break. An entire week of togetherness." He squeezed her thigh muscle. "You are tough. No wrestling, that's for sure." He patted her arm muscle too, and shook his head.

Self-conscious, Rhee drew back. "Too much?"

"Never. I love your soul, Rhee, doesn't matter what you look like."

"How can I be mad at you?"

"Why would you want to be?"

He kissed her, making her forget, too.

"I was going to tell you something. About Morpheus."

"Have the Oneiroi been back, or bothering your sleep? What about mean old Selene?"

Rhee gave him a slight push while she laughed. "Mean old Selene?"

"She trapped those poor guys, all 'cause the short ugly one fell in love with her."

"And tried to steal her magic horses – without them, no moonlight."

"A man in love does desperate things."

"Oh yeah?"

"Yeah."

"Like what?"

Dane paused. "Like. I don't know, travel hundreds of miles every other weekend to be with his girl. When are you gonna come visit me, Rhee?"

She stilled, realizing he had a point. Yet her words were defensive. "I am not the one that moved."

He physically pulled back from her. "Like I had a choice?"

"Wait," Rhee said, putting her hand against his chest. She'd learned from Selene that saying sorry was kinder than holding a grudge. "I know you bend over backward to see me. And your dad, too. I would love to come during the summer for a week or so, and see your place. Can I?"

Dane's expression transferred from hurt to joy. "Duh, Rhee. That would be really cool. Will the parents go for it?"

She tapped his heart. "Without question."

"I felt really bad for Phantasos. He totally and completely loved her."

"It was rotten luck that she was already in love, with her human. She made a deal with Hypnos, bringing her to Phantasos' attention. He never had a chance to gain Selene's regard, since she already loved the other guy."

"Still sucked." Dane lifted Rhee's hand and kissed each fingertip.

"Yeah, no argument there."

"Speaking of suckage, how did Melody do, meeting her dad?"

"Yikes! I need to call her. She seemed totally fine a few days ago, but you never know with Mel. She's super good at hiding her feelings."

"After her help with the dream catchers, I'm guessing she'll be more receptive to her psychic side."

"She decided to change, and she did. Pretty amazing." Rhiannon, proud of her friend, hoped Melody's dreams came true in a big way. She deserved it. "I got a post card from the rain forest, from J.W.. He said he had a dream that the Oneiroi were free from their curse."

"Where do you think the spirits are now?"

"Heaven, or the ancient Greek equivalent of it." Rhee shrugged then pulled him in for a hug, body to body, transferring all of the love she had to give.

"I wish we had answers." His hands smoothed her hair down her back.

"I'm beginning to think there are none. That life is this journey we agreed to take, to learn certain lessons." She fidgeted in his arms. "No easy answers, just lots and lots of questions."

Dane lifted her chin and stared into her eyes. "I feel your despondency, and your resilient hope. I feel your love for me, and return it ten times over. I want the rainbows you want, even though you deny it. I want the security and goodness for the world, like you."

"It isn't possible," Rhiannon said, resting her head against his chest. "There are too many Janets and Felicitys out there."

"It is possible. You know why?"

Rhiannon looked at him, too, desperately wanting to hear something she could hold on to. "No."

"Because, as you keep pointing out, we are what we want to be. We make the rules. You, Rhiannon Godfrey, could change the world with all that good stuff in your heart."

"Forget it Dane. No rainbows. And I don't believe in unicorns, either."

"I know what you feel, Rhiannon." He dropped a kiss to the tip of her nose. "Yes, you do."

ABOUT THE AUTHOR

Award-winning author Traci Hall is multi published in genre fiction for adults and teens. She lives near the beach in South Florida.

Find Traci online at:
TraciHall.com
Twitter.com/TraciHallAuthor
Facebook.com/Traciella

www.ingramcontent.com/pod-product-compliance
Lightning Source LLC
Chambersburg PA
CBHW070913180626
46817CB00003B/1044